SEARCH FOR
A NEW DAWN

Barbara Delinsky

This title first published in Great Britain 2003 by
SEVERN HOUSE PUBLISHERS LTD of
9–15 High Street, Sutton, Surrey SM1 1DF.
A paperback edition of this book was published
in the USA only in 1982 by Silhouette Books,
a division of Simon & Schuster, Inc. under the
pseudonym of Billie Douglass.
This title first published in the USA 2004 by
SEVERN HOUSE PUBLISHERS INC of
595 Madison Avenue, New York, N.Y. 10022.

British Library Cataloguing in Publication Data

Delinsky, Barbara, 1945-
    Search for a new dawn
    1.   Yukon Territory - Fiction
    2.   Love stories
    I.   Title   II. Douglass, Billie, 1945-
    813.5'4 [F]

ISBN 0-7278-6025-9

Except where actual historical events and characters are being
described for the storyline of this novel, all situations in this
publication are fictitious and any resemblance to living persons
is purely coincidental.

Printed and bound in Great Britain by
MPG Books Ltd., Bodmin, Cornwall.

To ERD, my firstborn

Dear Reader,

This book is labeled "A Classic Novel of Love" because it is indeed "a classic," originally published in 1982, and a "novel of love," shorter and narrower in scope than my more recent novels.

It was originally written under the Billie Douglass pseudonym. Since readers now know my real name, I am using that on this reissue. The only other change you will find is the cover design. The title is the original one, as is the story within.

I hope you enjoy reading *Search for a New Dawn* both as much as I enjoyed writing it, and as much as I enjoy rereading it today.

Barbara Delinsky

one

IT COULD HAVE BEEN ANY TAVERN IN ANY TOWN. The lights were low and orange, the air smoke-tinged, the steady drone of conversational mumblings disturbed only by the faint sound of the television from its perch high above the cordon of filled and half-filled bottles lining long shelves behind the bar, or the occasional coming together of metal boot and hardwood floor as a new customer joined the others. For a weekday afternoon, the tables were surprisingly filled, their red-and-white-checked tablecloths, shabby at best, now rapidly wrinkling under the onslaught of elbows, fists, cans, glasses, ashtrays, and the incidental sloshing by a slightly tipsy patron.

The faces were mostly male, mostly hard. They reflected the times as they reflected the place. For this was Whitehorse, at the edge of the Canadian wilderness in the Yukon Territory. Long gone were the days of the gold-rush bonanza, when a man struck it rich in a single day. Rather, these men worked day after day, year after year, to support themselves and their families in one of the inevitably mine-related activities that supported the small northern community. Many were miners themselves, eking out a living in the painstaking search for zinc, lead, and copper; others were part of the tourism business, serving the increasing numbers of travelers who clamored north to relive those days in 1898 when now-legendary adventurers by the tens of thousands poured into the area in search of El Dorado.

The hands that raised frothy steins were, by and large, worn and calloused—with the notable exception of one pair, in a far corner of the room. Young, delicately tanned, and distinctly feminine, they were clasped tightly around a steaming mug of coffee, their owner so totally engrossed in her own thoughts that she did not hear the approach of heavily shuffling footsteps.

"C'n I buy y'a drink, swee-heart?" The gravel-edged voice, slurred with drink and reeking likewise not six inches from her face, brought Rory Matthews's sandy head up with a start, and she as quickly recoiled from the gray face that hovered menacingly above her.

"No!" she refused forcefully, indignant that this derelict should approach her in the first place and unable to disguise the revulsion which swept over her at his grubby nearness.

"Wha-smatter?" he slurred on. "Not good'nough fur ya?"

Her better judgment, in a rare appearance, dictating that she not aggravate the man, Rory tempered her tone and ventured an excuse. "I'm waiting for someone." She had spoken no less than the truth, though when her brother might arrive was a question which any one of the strangers in the bar might have been better able to answer than she. He would certainly have received her message earlier today, or so she had been assured by the Mountie who sent it over the radio. Whether he would be able to leave right away to fetch her—whether he would *want* to leave right away—was an entirely different matter. Oh, yes, she certainly was waiting for someone, but it could be a very long wait. To her dismay, the miner, or so she guessed him to be from his garb, was oblivious to her hint.

"Aw, c'mon. Lemme look t'yer perty face a li'l longer." This was unthinkable; if her brother wasn't already furious at her, he certainly would be, to walk into the bar and find her having a drink with a significantly sloshed local. As he reached for the empty chair beside her, she spoke again, anger now rising above the frustration and indignation at being saddled with this pest.

"I'd rather be alone." Her green eyes bored into him, cold and imperious, as all traces of patience vanished.

"Humph! Hotsy-totsy r'ya? Too good fur th'likes o'me, d'ya think? Well-ll, we'll see bou'that." He grabbed her hair before she knew what had happened, and painfully yanked her up out of her chair, her head strained back, his slobbering lips on the descent—when, just as suddenly, she was released. Thick tawny lashes opened wide in astonishment as the man was sent sprawling onto the floor, having been bodily lifted and hurled by another of whose approach she had been unaware.

"Get that man home!" a deep voice commanded several of the other men who had watched the incident from start to finish, as had indeed the majority of the customers, Rory now embarrassingly noticed. Two burly men immediately lifted their friend and safely escorted him outside, as the tall one, who had so gallantly come to her aid, now turned to her for the first time.

Visibly shaken by the experience, Rory could muster no words, but merely glanced toward the stranger, as she unsteadily sat down again and reached up to rub the back of her head, still smarting from the drunkard's grip. Never had she had an experience such as this before. Her slightest whim had always been heeded; unwanted attention had just never presented itself in her sheltered existence.

"Are you all right, miss?" The voice was as velvet smooth as the amber eyes that gazed down at her. She nodded, still unable to speak, as a delayed reaction of trembling set in. The man searched her face a moment longer, then raised several fingers to summon the already approaching waitress. "Two white wines. You *do* have white wine, don't you?" The question, directed to the waitress, suggested that this man was no more a regular patron of the tavern than was Rory.

"Yes, sir." The girl nodded, scurrying off toward the bar, as the tall man helped himself to the free chair and Rory finally recovered her tongue.

"Thank you," she began softly, not overly accustomed to expressing gratitude and feeling mildly awkward at doing so. "That was frightening."

The man's expression became one of amusement. "Does white wine mean that much to you?" he mocked.

"I'm not talking about the wine," she snapped, instantly annoyed that her gesture had missed its mark. "That man . . . he came on so . . ." She looked down at her fingers, thin and tapered, wrapped tensely about the coffee mug.

"What are you doing here?" The tone of voice was firm and accusing as the eyes studied her.

"What do you mean?" she asked, raising her face defiantly to his. She had begun this trip in an attitude of independence, and despite the setback moments earlier, she would likewise continue. No stranger would put her down.

"A young girl like you shouldn't be sitting alone in a hole like this." His amber orbs held her green ones, as she willed herself not to flinch under their pressure.

"And just why not?" Her brow furrowed slightly in a mild show of anger at his implication.

"You are shaking in your boots. Need I tell you the facts of life?" he mocked again.

Suddenly her anger was thoroughly aroused. "*You* don't have to tell me a damn thing. Now, if you'll excuse—"

"Sit down and relax," he ordered calmly but insistently, a large, tanned hand reaching out to her forearm, keeping her in her seat. "I'm neither drunk nor a molester of the undesirous. Rest assured you are in safe hands."

Incensed, she stared at the hand that restrained her. "Let go of me!"

His eyes narrowed and his voice lowered, as he mimicked the words she had heard not long ago: "What's the matter? Not good enough for you?"

A shudder passed through her at the reminder, yet she found herself at a loss to respond. Glaring intently at the man, she wondered whether she had, in fact, been saved from the frying pan only to be tossed into the fire. For the stranger before her was far from the attentive, indulging companion she was used to. He was, as she had noted from the first, tall and lean, the broad shoulders of his open jacket tapering to a slimness at the waist and hips, pure muscle poured into faded denims, disappearing into worn leather boots below the knee. His hair was straight, full and dark, practically black, with a sheen to it that even the dim lights of the tavern brought forth. He was bearded, though not heavily, the black growth trimmed respectably, lending the air of the adventurer to what would otherwise, she guessed, be a stern face. He was the epitome of the dark and mysterious frontiersman, his deep amber eyes as compelling in their spirit as the red wool cap, absently crammed into a back pocket, the only touch of bright color amid his otherwise sober garb.

"You are staring. Is it annoyance or fascination?" he questioned her, humor etched into lines radiating from the corners of his eyes. If the truth were told, the latter would be the case, though it was far from the time of truth.

"Don't flatter yourself," she retorted. "I just wondered who was preferable, you or that man you just ousted."

He seemed to enjoy the banter, sparkles flickering through the smooth amber. "Patience, patience. You'll discover that soon enough." He glanced up quickly as the wine arrived, accompanied by a honey-eyed look from the waitress, whose arm quite conveniently brushed against his shoulder as she placed the glasses on the table.

"Will that be all for now?" she crooned indecently into his ear, and Rory could no longer ignore the intimacy.

"My God, they certainly make them provocative around here," she commented wryly, when a nod of her companion's head had curtly sent the offender off toward another table.

"You shouldn't talk, young lady." The eyes were on her once again, this time appraising her from shoulder to toe, as he leaned sideways to take in what the table hid. "That's quite an outfit you're wearing," he drawled, his eyes catching the rosy glow that had involuntarily sprung to her cheeks.

"What's wrong with it?" Defiance burst out anew. She had taken pains in shopping for this trip, purchasing clothes that promised to be both stylish and—in her sadly naïve judgment—appropriate. Her jeans were tight fitting and embroidered strategically with gold threads, whose warmth was echoed by the western-style, open-necked cotton shirt that lay beneath her denim Eisenhower jacket, also gold-trimmed and perfectly coordinated with the lightest strands of her sandy hair as it fell gently about her shoulders. Yes, she rather liked the outfit she had donned very, very early that morning, ages ago it seemed, when she had left her home in Seattle, taken a jet to Vancouver, then another on to Whitehorse.

"Those clothes may be very smart for wherever *you* come from," he explained, "but among these people"—he gestured at the modestly dressed group in the tavern—"they stick out like a sore thumb. But then"—he looked at her thoughtfully, his own thumb moving slowly back and forth across the hair bordering his upper lip—"maybe that was what you had in mind."

The man had a way of infuriating her with every sentence, crumbling her desire to remain cool and suave. Now she spoke between clenched teeth, keeping her voice low to avoid another public display of her inability to handle the male species. "What was, or is, in my mind is none of your business. I *do* find you as offensive as that boozer. I wouldn't have a drink with him, and I don't believe I'll have a drink with you." She had reached over to pick up her pocketbook, when strong fingers again stopped her.

"You told your, ah, admirer that you were waiting for someone." The face was now completely serious, the eyes magnetizing hers. "If that's true, then I'll stay with you until he comes. If not, let me take you someplace else. These men are no saints." Her glance followed his to the audience of eager eyes around them, then, with a start, she drew her gaze back to him.

"And you are?" she retorted angrily, acutely aware of his fingers on her arm, searing like a brand through her jacket and the cool cotton beneath.

"No, I'm not. But I'm not quite as starved for it as they may be." His implication was obvious, and although he had been entirely serious and not in the least mocking, Rory took offense at his words.

"What in the devil are *you* . . . the Playboy of the Western World?" As soon as the words were out, she wondered if she had gone too far. She soon knew that she had.

The hand on her arm moved down to take her fingers, as the dark head moved closer. "Get your bag and come with me. Do not make a scene, or you will have any number of these men at your service. I am taking you out of here and somewhere a little more safe. Now, get up." His voice was commanding, yet strangely nonthreatening. Never having been confronted like this before, Rory complied.

Her first shock came as the strong arm drew her to her feet, and its owner casually straightened to his full height. If he hadn't already given her sufficient grounds for intimidation, he certainly did now. For Rory found herself positively dwarfed by this man who had taken charge of her. He had to be at least six three; never before had she felt so insignificant, a solid foot shorter, boot heels and all.

Deftly the stranger tossed some money onto the table in payment for the barely touched wine, as deftly tossed a wink at the waitress, most definitely for Rory's benefit more than the other's, and firmly guided her among the maze of tables and through the door of the tavern.

Why she was so docilely letting this man direct her, Rory did not know. She suspected that what he had said about the patrons of the tavern may well have been true, however, and as humiliated as she felt at being dictated to so condescendingly, there was a certain relief at leaving the heavy atmosphere of the bar behind and stepping out into the temporarily blinding brightness of the day. Once on the sidewalk, the pressure of the hand at her elbow eased, and although Rory knew she was free to walk off, something held her.

"What *were* you doing in there?" he repeated the question that had gone unanswered earlier, as they slowly walked down the street.

"Having some coffee."

"Coffee? In a bar?" he countered skeptically. It was only when she stopped still in her tracks and turned to squint up at him that she saw the humor that had returned to his eyes.

"Yes. Coffee. In a *tavern*. At least, it was billed as a tavern by the hotel clerk. I saw no reason nót to go there." She had indignantly taken her elbow from his hand as she jerked around to move forward again. She did not have to glance sideways to feel him easily matching her short stride.

"Have you seen the river?" He deftly changed the subject. As she shook her head, he took her elbow once again and propelled her gently toward the pier.

"This was quite a spot in the days of the gold rush. Whitehorse saw many a potential prospector set off on the river, never to make it even through the canyon six miles up!"

"You seem very familiar with the town," she ventured. "You're not a miner." She looked him in the eye, daring him to pronounce her wrong.

"How can you tell?" he returned in amusement.

"Your hands. They're too smooth. You have no calluses." She had noted that immediately, just as she had the wisps of dark hair on his forearm, exposed where his shirt sleeve had been rolled back over the cuff of his wool jacket. But of course she wouldn't tell him about that particular observation, which had nothing at all to do with mining.

"Very observant," he commented, raising an eyebrow as though reading her thoughts. "What else?"

"What else, what?" She played dumb.

"What other brilliant deductions have you made about me?"

She held his gaze as boldly as she knew how. "That you are arrogant enough to assume that I would be 'fascinated'—to use your word—by you." Then, to her immediate chagrin, she betrayed herself thoroughly. "What *do* you do?" Her companion broke into an uncontrolled guffaw, as she chided herself for her impulsiveness. But she had gone too far to retreat. "Well, what *do* you do here? Oh," she continued, interrupting herself as she thought aloud, "you don't live here either, do you?"

He laughed again at her chatter. "So there *was* something else you picked up. No, I don't live here. I'm on my vacation."

"How do you know so much about this area?" she persisted.

"I've been here before. And I read. Don't you?" His accusation was subtle, though direct. As she watched him talk, she saw for the first time the firmness of his lips, which dominated, rather than being hidden by, his beard.

Once again fearing that he'd suspected the truth, she retaliated sharply. "Of course I do!" But she'd never had particular cause to read for pusposes such as this, when there was always someone at her elbow, as he was now, to tell her what she needed to know. She had indeed been pampered all her life. Reading was merely a requirement for education, something that one did to complete a course and get a passing grade. Or, such had been her understanding until she'd met Charles Dwyer and had discovered that one could spend an entire evening, alone yet not alone, thoroughly enthralled by the printed word.

Only now did it occur to her that she could—and should—have done some research before this trip. And the fact that she hadn't was ample reminder of how far she had yet to go. She'd had ten days to prepare for the journey, yet, reverting to habit, she'd thought more of clothes than information. Guilt washed over her at the realization that she was in a strange town, knowing nothing about it other than that her brother would soon be here to take over. But, she argued in silent self-accusation, that was exactly what she had wanted to avoid. She wanted to act on her own, to be self-sufficient, to behave like an adult not a coddled child, hidden from life's potential threats.

"Powerful, isn't it?" His words, soft and low as they were, tore into her thoughts as her wandering mind's eyes riveted to the waters of the Yukon River, lying just before them. She gasped audibly, astonished at the ruggedness of nature's force. Steadily swirling along on its northwest course, the water changed, chameleonlike, from pea-green to navy, held staunchly in check by steep sandy banks rising straight up from the shore, the gray of rocky cliffs high above dotted with the green of the fir and the blue of the spruce.

"Yes," she murmured in quiet agreement, as she appreciated the sight for a while longer. It was a dramatic change from the luxury of Ácapulco, the elegance of the Riviera, or the opulence of the Caribbean islands, through which she had cruised more than once. Her brother had turned down the lure of those lush spots for this rugged land; in this short instant, she could almost understand why.

This land *demanded* from its inhabitants. She could see that in the anger of the swirling waters. The other places she had visited gave willingly, gave unconditionally, then gave some more. This land, she sensed, was different. If she were to accompany her brother farther into this wilderness—and she was absolutely determined to do so—she sensed that her mettle would be sorely tested before she returned once again to this spot. A shiver ran through her, as she wondered if, indeed, she possessed the strength she so desperately needed to find within herself.

"Cold?" Once again he interrupted her thoughts, this tall stranger who had, in essence, begun her on her journey.

"No," she answered, quickly recovering from the surprise at bouncing back from her daydream to find him at her side. "I was . . . just thinking." He studied her fair features for a moment, catching the last trace of vulnerability quivering at her lip, before her mask of self-assurance fell into place once more. He cocked his head away from the river.

"Come on. Let's go back." As they turned, he threw a casual arm over her shoulder. An hour earlier, she would have promptly and haughtily cast it off as the gesture of an impertinent fellow making fast time with her. Now, to her puzzlement, she let it stay, as she had the hand at her elbow earlier. Somehow, in the face of the future, which frightened her even as it beckoned so strongly, she needed the comfort of that strong arm, guiding her, if only back to her hotel.

"You haven't told me your name," he accused her gently, as they entered the door of the inn where she was staying. She felt neither smug nor indifferent in this man's presence and saw no reason to hide her identity from him.

"Rory. Rory Matthews."

"Rory Matthews? What kind of a name is that?" he exclaimed incredulously. She turned slowly to stare at him open-mouthed. What could she say? It was indeed her name. Granted, she had taken her mother's maiden name when her parents had been divorced and her mother had done so, but it *was* her legal name. "Rory Matthews . . ." he repeated, as Rory's anger blossomed. "Rory Matthews . . . you've got to be an aspiring movie star." His eyes raked her length. "Too short to be a model."

That did it! "It just so happens that Rory Matthews is my real name and has been so for many years." It was the old Rory, back again with the fury of an offended princess. Hastily retrieving her key from her pocketbook, she started to mount the stairs to her second-floor room, then paused and turned to the man whose eyes were above hers even though he stood two steps below. "I hope you've had an amusing afternoon for yourself," she sniped sarcastically as she turned on her heel and proceeded up the stairs, intent on looking only forward. Indignantly, she stalked down the hallway, shabbily carpeted in a rust color that matched the worn wallpaper hanging on either side. Her key had barely touched the lock when two hands hit the wall on either side of her, and she whirled to find herself imprisoned by the man from whom she assumed she had made a regal escape.

"What do you want?" she growled, her head tilted sharply up to meet his gaze.

"You haven't thanked me properly," he mocked, the intensity of his amber eyes belying the smile on his lips.

"Thanked you for what?" she spat out, the venom in her voice oddly diluted by the jelly feeling in her knees and the accelerated beat of her pulse.

"Rescuing you in the, ah, tavern . . . showing you the town." His breath fanned over her in a not unpleasant way, and Rory looked desperately around for a means of escape from this magnetism. "You wondered who was better . . . that drunken miner or me?" He left no more time to wonder as his lips descended on hers, gentle yet firm, commanding yet inviting. Every rational instinct told her to repel this presumptuous stranger, yet she found herself unable to move. No part of their bodies touched but their lips, as his proceeded on the route of sensual persuasion to coax hers into response. She felt the surprisingly soft and seductive rub of his beard against her face, smelled the earthy male scent of him slowly but surely drugging her senses. His subtlety created a headiness of its own, and she found her lips beginning to return his play, instinctively craving more than the teasing pressure offered. It was a wholly new experience for her—sensing, feeling, desiring, giving, for the pure beauty of the moment.

"Rory! What in the hell's going on here . . .?" An angry voice shattered the aura as a figure appeared on the threshold of the door, which had opened from the inside, unnoticed by either of the pair in the hallway. Rory recognized the voice in an instant, the knowledge wrenching her from her dazed state as she whirled to confront the infuriated face of her brother.

"Daniel! I didn't know you were here!" she exclaimed breathlessly, her knees weaker than ever, but now for a different reason.

"That was obvious!" he snarled. "I was wondering when you'd bother to check in here, you numbskull! Who in the devil is this character?" he barked savagely, grabbing her arm possessively as he looked from his sister to the man she had been kissing so passionately.

The latter, having drawn himself up straight, was as busily eyeing the two, a look of faint amusement shaping his features. Having reached some tentative conclusion, he directed his gaze to Rory. To her utter amazement, he bent his head forward, placed a gentle kiss on her cheek, then lifted a thumb to briefly touch her lips. "Thank you." His voice was soft and gentle. Then he turned, and before either onlooker could react to his gutsy performance, he was gone.

Daniel, the first to recover, dragged her into the room and slammed the door shut behind him. "All right, little sister, I want you to tell me what's going on," he seethed, as she unconsciously walked to the window in time to see a tall figure disappear down the street. "Rory! I'm talking to you! What are you doing here?"

Slowly gathering her thoughts, she turned to face her brother, whose normally gentle features were now coiled in tension. She had always adored him, particularly after their mother's death six years ago when he, a full twelve years her senior, had taken her under his wing and become mother, father, brother, and friend to her. Now he stood before her, his height and build average, his hair brown and vaguely similar in texture to her own, dressed in the rough work clothes of an on-the-spot reporter on assignment in the Canadian backwoods, awaiting an explanation for her sudden and unexpected appearance. "Rory." His voice revealed his growing impatience, and he placed a hand on his hip, a favorite stance of his, "I'm waiting. . . ."

"I've got to *do* something, Dan," she began. "I'm bored and frustrated and . . . I'm coming with you."

"What? I'm on an assignment, Rory. You know that," he countered angrily. "There's no place for you there."

"Oh, come on, Dan. You can find something for me to do. I won't be in the way," she pleaded, moving closer to him as she pursued her argument.

"Rory, you have no idea what I am involved in. It's out of the question." He shook his head to reinforce his words. "I'm sorry, sweetie." His tone was that of the big brother looking after her best interests. In the past it had always silenced her. Now, however, it had the opposite effect.

Petulance came to the fore as Rory reacted to the refusal she had indeed feared. Stamping her foot, she stormed, "You are not sorry. Don't patronize me. You are a bigot. A damned bigot! You think I can't cope with your wilderness. What's so tough about the mountains? I'll be able to keep up. I'm in great condition!" She pulled herself up a little straighter as though to reinforce her words.

Her brother looked down in amusement. "Great condition, sure. For swimming the length of the pool ten times, for staying on the dance floor or the tennis court 'til all hours of the morning. You're right, Rory. You are in great condition. But not for this kind of work."

"I don't see the difference," she scoffed.

"Of course you don't," Daniel agreed, his tone softening as he gently put his hands on her shoulders. "Rory, you have lived a very, very comfortable life. Mother wanted it that way, I want it that way, and you have always been happy that way. You have everything you could ever need or want. Challenge to you is a game, not a potentially dangerous situation. Up here, it can very well become a matter of survival. The life in the wilderness is tough. There are no servants, no swimming pools, no tennis courts, no beauty shops or fancy restaurants, no feather beds. There are sleeping bags on hard floors or the damp ground, mosquitoes and black flies, cold weather, physical exertion day after day, nourishment out of a can more often than not . . ."

"Why do *you* do it?" She cornered him, suspecting that he could make her point for her.

He dropped his hands from their gentle caress of her shoulders and walked to the window to stare out over the street. "Touché," he murmured. She smiled with smug satisfaction as her brother ventured to elaborate. "I love my work. It offers variety. It offers challenge. This summer it is covering the glaciologists beyond Ross River. Next fall it will be something else." He turned back to face her, imploring her to understand. He had always been truthful with her, on that she could count. "I like the wilderness, Rory. The social whirl at home tires me and bores me, more than tramping for days through the backwoods ever could. But I'm a man. I can thrive on the rigors of this kind of life. I want something easier for you."

Rory felt her resistance weaken under such heartfelt concern, but she, too, had begun to recognize certain unfulfilled needs. "What about me? Doesn't it matter what I want? Dan, can't you see that I want something more just like you do? You really are a male chauvinist if you think I can't cope with some hardship. But then," she thought aloud, absently tucking a tawny curl behind her ear, "you've all coddled me so much that maybe I can't cope."

She looked down at the floor, trying to control the anger that was once again on the upsurge. When she gazed at her brother, there was more than a little bitterness in her green eyes. "I had a whole new experience today, Dan. I was in a tavern, which the clerk downstairs had been so good as to recommend," she began, a sarcastic touch to her words. "A drunk approached me and wanted to sit down. Needless to say, I put him off in my usual manner. The only thing was, he didn't much care for my usual manner. So help me, I think he would have raped me, he was that angry. Fortunately, there were other people in the bar, although only one came to my aid." She paused, noting the fury simmering in her brother's eyes.

"You crazy little girl!" he stormed, shocking her that *she* should bear the brunt of his anger rather than the drunk. "You see, you should never have come here! You can't even handle passing strangers in a bar!"

Her anger quickly matched his. "That's just the point. I've never had to. Everything has always been so easy, so taken care of. Daniel, I want to be able to take care of myself. I don't want to be dependent on people to protect me all my life." The flare of temper, which had faded with her words, disappeared entirely beneath the searching gaze of her brother.

Deep in thought, he studied her, at once puzzled and concerned, then finally ventured to voice his thoughts. "What's happened, Rory? You've been very content until now, or so I thought. Why the sudden change?"

Rory looked quickly away as memory evoked a kaleidoscope of embarrassment, pleasure, awakening, and understanding. She'd never mentioned Charles before to him. Did she have the courage now? The experience, while proving to be a turning point in her life, had begun with such a mortifying twist. Unsure yet as to what she would say, she hedged softly, gazing off toward the window to escape her brother's probing stare. "It's not all that sudden. It's just been . . . something within me . . . building up over the past year. . . ."

There was a flicker of suspicion and even more of anxiety in Daniel's response. "What kind of 'something'? Did you get into some kind of trouble? Are you running away from something?"

"No!" she exclaimed emphatically, then softened once again as she realized both that she had, by past behavior, justifiably brought his suspicion on herself, and that Daniel *would,* in the end, demand his explanation, if he were to allow her to go back with him into the wilderness. "I met someone . . . he made me see things differently." When the anticipated retort from her brother never materialized, Rory sat down on the bed and began to explain.

"I did something really foolish last fall." She spoke quickly, eager to confess her folly and thereby put it finally behind her. "I'd signed up for a creative-writing course at the university, only to discover that the professor was new, very good-looking, very mature, and from all outward appearances, very available. I'd never dated a professor and the thought was . . . well, exciting. So, I sought him out." A rose flush brushed her cheeks as she recalled that her behavior, in hindsight, was both childish and humiliating.

"Oh, I was vaguely subtle about the whole thing," she defended herself feebly. "I made a point to 'need' his help, over and over again, in my work. And he seemed to like it, to enjoy helping me, to be pleasantly amused by my attentions. He asked me question after question about myself—many of which I could not answer, since they involved a depth of thought I'd systematically avoided before." One glance at Daniel's taut features prompted her to elaborate further.

"His questions were perfectly natural, since the writing for the course was primarily on self-directed topics, experiential, some strictly autobiographical. At the time"—she laughed softly at her naïveté—"I thought Charles was interested in me personally."

"Did he ever ask you out?"

"No. Well, not really."

The beginnings of impatience tinged Daniel's urgings. "'Not really'? Now what's that supposed to mean?" He still expected a typically irresponsible Rory-type outcome to this story, and could therefore not understand its long-drawn-out nature.

Standing, she slowly walked around the room, coming to rest with her back braced against the door, facing her brother's intent gaze. "*I* asked *him* out first. He refused, and naturally that made me all the more determined to snag him. After all"—she smirked in self-deprecation—"I'd *never* been turned down before. When I asked a second time, he turned around and invited me to _his_ place for dinner." Her voice broke off as her mind conjured up the image of that apartment, small and simple, and as emotionally warm as anything she'd ever imagined.

"Go on."

Returning quickly to her narrative, Rory continued. "That dinner, Dan, was one I'll never forget. It was the most interesting, most stimulating, most enjoyable evening I'd ever had—after my initial shock."

"Shock?"

A gentle smile softened her lips. "There were just the three of us—Charles, myself . . . and Monica."

"Monica?" Incredulity had begun to build as Daniel sensed that he, too, was in for a surprise. He was correct.

"His wife." The bombshell exploded no less thunderously in Daniel's mind than it had in Rory's when she'd first been introduced to Monica.

"His wife? What kind of kinky—"

Rory broke in with a smile of understanding. "Nothing kinky, Daniel. Monica is a fantastic girl. She and Charles are very happily, and traditionally, married. And, in a way, my impression had been correct. Charles _did_ like me, just as I liked him. But purely as a friend . . . and as someone he thought Monica might enjoy." Daniel's still-bewildered expression goaded her on. "You see, they'd just moved to Seattle from the East Coast. Monica is only two years older than I am and hadn't made many friends yet. We've become very close."

"So there was nothing sexual—"

"No!" Rory's impatience flared momentarily, before she chuckled softly. "I think Charles thoroughly enjoyed my discomfort when he first brought me into their apartment. There was no way I could be angry with him. I'd cooked my own goose!"

Daniel hesitated a moment, trying to put the pieces of the puzzle together. "I'm not sure I understand, Rory. What is the connection between your acquaintance with Charles and Monica . . . and your sudden change of heart regarding life?"

Overlooking the faint sarcasm in his voice, she explained. "Charles and Monica are like no other people I've ever known. They work hard. He teaches, she is fluent in Spanish and does some free-lance translating and interpreting. They struggle to make ends meet and then just begin to taste some of the luxuries we take for granted. Yet they are happier than any couple I've met. They love each other. Each is self-sufficient, all the while getting a very special something from the other." Whether Daniel's reflections were on the relationship of their own parents, so different from what she'd just described and so abortive, she couldn't tell. Yet she felt more confident now, assured by her brother's expression that he was listening and hearing her.

"I've spent a lot of time with them, both with Monica, alone, and with the two as a couple. I've helped Monica cook and wash dishes—yes, *me,* wash dishes. Believe it or not, Dan, when Monica threw her back out and was in bed for a week, *I* kept their household running. Oh, Monica told me just what to do, and Charles is far from helpless, but I actually did the cooking, the cleaning, the marketing, the laundry. *Me!*" A justifiable pride poured forth in her words, followed by an element of unmistakable surprise. "And I *enjoyed* it! I felt important, useful. If I hadn't seen the look of pain on Monica's face with each muscle spasm, I might have suspected that the two of them had plotted my impromptu education. They were patient and encouraging, then overwhelmingly appreciative. I found that it was rewarding to do things for others, for a change!"

Pausing to catch her breath, Rory's eyes brightened anew at the thought of her friends. "We've had many deep discussions. They like me as a person— for no other reason. Money, looks, social status, background—these things mean very little to the Dwyers. And I envy them! They live so simply, yet they're very happy. . . ." Her voice trailed off as her story reached its conclusion. There was no need to tell Daniel of those conversations during which, for the first time in her life, she'd felt totally inferior. They had never criticized her for her sheltered past. Rather, it was the contrast between her past and theirs, and the very differences between their present life-styles, which had left its mark on her.

Once again, her thoughts were interrupted by Daniel's voice, now quiet and even. "So you'd like to live simply . . . and find happiness?"

Rory shot him a look of frustration, fearing that he still refused to take her seriously. "No. I'd like to do something more meaningful than what I've done in the past." A coy curve feather-touched the corners of her lips. "You have to admit that my interests have been rather shallow. . . ."

Her self-evaluation was met only by a raised eyebrow, which was lowered as quickly in silent agreement and perhaps the slightest hint of admiration. But then, to Rory's surprise, her brother stood and moved toward the window, his back to her, his voice again tense when he finally broke the silence. "What can I say? I agree with your ends, though I disagree with your means. Must you go from one extreme to the other?"

Innocence flooded her green eyes. "But I haven't done that. *You're* here. I have you to guide me. That's why I came."

"I was wondering about that," he said wryly. "You're as naïve as you ever were, Rory. You have no idea what it takes to live in the wilderness. I can assure you it's quite different from your friends' apartment!"

"Then teach me!" she shot back, adding as a bitter afterthought, "You helped spoil me, now you can help undo that damage. You helped make me totally dependent, now help me to be self-reliant. Let me *do* things. Let me be your assistant and help with your work. Don't you see," she pleaded softly, "if I can get started with you, I can then branch out on my own. But I have to prove to *myself* that I can do it, before I have to prove it to others. If I can't ask *your* help, whose can I ask?"

With a sigh of frustration, Daniel looked at her askance. "You'd have any number of eligible young men clamoring to help you," he joked dryly. "And, by the way, who was that guy out in the hall? What kind of a scene was that?"

The subject changed abruptly. As Rory's thoughts returned to the tall stranger, she felt a warmth creep upward to her lips, which his had caressed so sensually. Praying that her brother would not notice her blush, she explained. "He was the one who came to my aid in the bar."

"Came to your aid? For what? So that he could take advantage of you himself?" he snapped testily. "That was quite some kiss."

Now Rory knew that the color in her cheeks would betray her, but she made a token show of nonchalance. "It was only a kiss." She quickly turned her back, feigning annoyance at his prodding as she recalled what was "only a kiss." Despite its simplicity, it had been the most complex kiss she had ever in her life received. No, received was the wrong word, telling only half the story, she knew; for, in the end, she had given as well.

"What was his name?" Her brother's question was innocent enough, Rory's heartbeat screeched to a halt before resuming double time. The silence was deafening. "Rory, who was he?" Again, the growing impatience.

"I don't know." There. It was barely audible, yet loud enough to shock him. Or was she in fact the one who was the most shocked by this realization?

Daniel eyed her incredulously. "You don't know? You stand in the hallway of a hotel making out with some guy and you don't even know his name?"

Rory whirled around to face him. "No," she repeated, loudly and forcefully this time, "I don't know his name." Little did Daniel suspect that her anger was directed more at the tall stranger and at herself, for having overlooked this small detail, than at her brother.

"And that, young lady," Daniel concluded with the aplomb of a journalist, "is why you'll be going home on the first plane out of here tomorrow morning."

Instinctively, Rory knew that her brother would hear no more argument for the moment. She had learned only too well from past experience that he did not like anyone tampering with his final sentence. She had no intention of returning on any plane in the morning, but there would be a better time for argument later. Instead, she watched as Daniel scooped up his jacket. "Where are you going?"

There was more than a hint of impatience in his

eye when he turned from the door to answer her. "Believe it or not, Aurora Matthews, I got the message that you had shown up only *after* I got into Whitehorse. I came in for supplies, which I'm now about to pick up, and I would have spent the night anyway. So, you see, this is your lucky day," he added mischievously. "My wrath would have been ten times greater had I made a special trip down from the site just to turn you around and send you home."

Rory bit her lip to silence the many retorts that begged to be voiced. His wrath, indeed! She would learn to live with his wrath if that was the only way she could escape the swaddling clothes he had wrapped her in for the last twenty-one years! She was going to the site of the glacier, whether her brother liked it or not. Once and for all, she would see what it was that gave him the something "more" in his life that she so badly wanted in hers.

Yet Daniel was right in many ways. She had had everything she'd always wanted. She had gone to the finest schools, traveled extensively, first-class all the way, had been groomed for the cream of West Coast social life, had met all the "right" people, been to all the "right" places, done all the "right" things. It was primarily her exposure to Charles and Monica, still astounding in its effect on her, that had begun her wondering about exactly where she was headed.

Having finished a general liberal-arts course at the university, she had a degree but no career in sight or in mind. She had a social pedigree, as the daughter of the late great G. Arthur Turner and his first wife, the lovely Victoria Matthews, and an increasing disdain for the follies it entailed. She had the looks—petite and fair, sandy-haired and healthy-looking, curved in just the right places to show off the high-fashion clothing she customarily purchased. Oh, she had the looks, but what good did they do her when they merely attracted a long string of boring clingers, men enamored with her family's wealth and status far more than her own personal merits, if indeed she possessed any.

When she had made her preposterous play for Charles Dwyer, she was attracted first and foremost by his difference from the others she'd known. Even after the truth of his marriage had been thrust upon her, showing Charles to be indeed "unavailable," she grew to like and respect him more, her feelings for him augmented by those for his sincerely warm, down-to-earth wife, whom Rory now regarded as a very close friend.

In hindsight, she knew that, even aside from the fact of his own marriage, a man like Charles would never have seriously considered her as a wife. She had too little to offer! And it was this thought that hurt above all. Perhaps that was what her rebellion was about. She had to discover what lay within her, where it would take her, what she was truly meant for. Only then could she give a direction to her life. Only then could she have something of value to offer the man of her choice.

When her brother returned to the room, he was in an even poorer temper. Rory watched from the bed as he threw his jacket down beside her and began to pace the floor.

"Okay, what have I done now?" She sighed in resignation, fully expecting a new outburst against her arrival.

"Damn," he swore under his breath. "If it isn't one thing, it's the next. First, you show up here"—he sent her a menacing glance—"now this delay."

"What delay?"

He resumed his pacing. "The foundation that's sponsoring this expedition . . . its chairman is coming up to see it firsthand."

"How do you know?"

"The Mounties are quite good at relaying messages." He gave her a sharp glance, his undertone relating to her own escapade.

"So, what is the problem?"

"No problem . . . when the guy gets here. But I've got to sit around until he does." He ran a none-too-clean hand through his hair in a gesture of frustration. "I've just finished loading up the jeep so that I could get started first thing after you've left. Now I may have to wait for several more days."

"What supplies did you need?" Rory asked, as the germ of an idea began to take shape in her mind.

"Some film and other photographic material for Tony. Some canned goods, foodstuffs. And several pieces of climbing equipment. Nothing perishable, but everything needed . . . yesterday!"

Now he had her full and undivided attention as she bolted up. "Let *me* bring the supplies, Dan. I could at least be of some help! How difficult can driving to a site be?"

"Rory, Rory, Rory." He shook his head as though scolding a naughty child. "You have no idea of what these roads are like. They are pure gravel. Bumpy, rough, monotonous. At best, the trip can be made in five hours. At worst, fifteen. You can't drive over fifty miles an hour, under good conditions—"

She interrupted him excitedly. "I can do it, Dan! I

can handle the jeep. Don't forget—that little foreign job I drive at home has a stick and a clutch, too! I can help you. Won't that solve your problem? When this fellow arrives, you can rent a vehicle and drive him up. He'll need something to drive back in anyway."

Daniel smiled affectionately. For a minute, she thought she had won. "Sweetie, don't you see? Anything could happen out there on the road. What would you do if you had a breakdown? I can just see you changing a tire," he teased. "And what are you going to do if you *do* get there in one piece? There are five men out there, not counting myself and our benefactor. No one has the time, or desire, to wait on you," he added with a sympathetic smirk.

"No one has to," she snapped angrily. "I can make myself useful. I can take care of myself. Daniel, I'm going!" She tried a final time.

"No!" Had she been deaf in both ears, she would have felt the force of his response. Then, more quietly, he went on. "Let's go get some dinner. They may even have a movie in this town. Then you can get a good sleep. We'll head for the airport early tomorrow."

It was, indeed, very early the next morning when Daniel awoke. Tossing on some warm clothes to fend off the early chill, he left his room, crossed the hall to his sister's, and knocked on the door to awaken her. "Rory, it's me. Wake up."

No response. He knocked again, louder this time, only to be met with the same stony silence. "Rory?" Jiggling the handle, he discovered, much to his surprise in light of his orders to the contrary the previous evening, that the door was unlocked. Impatiently, he entered the room, prepared to chastise his sister for her carelessness. All too quickly he realized that his prospective audience was not in sight. "Rory!" he shouted toward the bathroom, flinging back its door. As he turned to see that indeed the bed had been slept in, his eye caught sight of the note that had been placed conspicuously atop the pillow. With a sigh of exasperation he began to read:

Dear Dan,
   Please don't be too angry. I have taken the jeep and headed for the site. Your map looked clear, so I doubt I'll have any trouble. Now you can relax for the few days until your man gets there, knowing that the supplies will have been safely delivered. I'm so glad to have something useful to do!
   All my love,
   Rory

   P.S. I won't let on that you are my brother. That way, if you are still displeased when you get to the site, you can completely disown me as some dimwitted crackpot! See you soon!

Slowly and wearily, Daniel folded the letter and tucked it into a pocket as he ran tense fingers through his sleep-disheveled hair. Damn, he swore silently, as he stalked back into his own room, slamming the door shut behind him. Then it occurred to him with a twinge of amusement that perhaps she had changed; the old Rory would never have been able to awaken before the sun!

two

IT WAS FAR FROM THE EASY RIDE THAT RORY HAD expected when she arose at dawn, having slept no more than two or three hours in her worry that Daniel would awaken early and thwart her plans. She had quickly repacked things which had been unpacked but hours before, and made her way to the jeep, which was parked behind the hotel in the small and surprisingly crowded parking lot. Fortunately, the clerk gave her no argument, trusting soul that he was, when he handed over the keys, which had been left at the desk by order of the management, in case a vehicle had to be moved during the night to allow passage of another. With the map beside her, taken from the back seat where she had scrutinized it the previous evening, she started out, stopping wisely at a gas station to assure the jeep its full tank, and at a coffee shop for a quick breakfast to assure herself of the same.

Driving the jeep proved to be the one groundless worry of the many that had plagued her during the

sleepless hours of the night. Fortunately, as she had
assured Daniel, she was well used to handling a manual transmission, complete with stick and clutch,
thanks to her own sporty version which transported
her from engagement to engagement at home. After
several minor bucks and jolts of adjustment to this
larger, less well-primed vehicle, she moved forward.
That was where the good news ended.

Granted, she had not anticipated a four-lane
superhighway, such as those to which she was
accustomed back home, particularly after Daniel's
warnings the day before. But neither had she anticipated the constant jostling that mile upon mile of
gravel-topped roadway could cause. Car sickness
was not her style, though she found herself squirm-
ing in her seat, trying to get comfortable behind the
wheel, within the first hour of this perverse torture.
The driving proved to be easier when she slowed to
a more sedate forty mph, though she knew that she
was adding more time onto her trip by doing so.

Fellow travelers were few and far between, which
was a mixed blessing. On the one hand, she worried
about being isolated should the jeep become disabled; on the other, she had been so terrified by the
storm of gravel that pelted her windshield when an
oncoming vehicle approached that she breathed a
sigh of relief at each empty stretch of the road.

The land, which progressively swallowed her up
in its vastness, seemed to possess a dual personality,
alternately mountains, then plateaus. The road followed the river for the most part, but took the path
of least resistance whenever possible. This meant
that she found herself making better than 250-degree
turns at some spots, before resuming the overall
northeasterly direction she wanted.

After an hour and a half of driving, Rory relaxed somewhat at the thought that she had come far enough to avoid an abrupt retrieval by her brother. Pulling the car over to the side of the road, she stepped out to stretch her muscles and give welcome respite to her backside, which had born the brunt of the abuse thus far.

Standing on a nearby ledge above the river, she was again struck by the rugged beauty and awesome power of the wilderness, epitomized by the river's relentless pounding against sheer walls of granite, which jutted straight up to support the flora of the countryside: the aspens and the spruce, the gleaming birches, the bouquets of wildflowers carpeting the high plateau. On a distant promontory stood a deserted cabin, once belonging perhaps to a trapper or a lone miner, whose life of solitude had since passed. Farther down the river, on a small sandy tract, she could make out the ruins of a boat, its hull battered by waters resentful of human intrusion.

Rory zipped her Eisenhower jacket higher as the wind suddenly picked up, sending murmurs through the tall firs. Taking a deep breath, she climbed behind the wheel once more, this time folding several layers of sweaters on the seat for a cushion. How lucky she was that Doris had insisted she bring extras!

Dear, dear Doris, mused Rory affectionately. She had served the family since Rory had been a baby, pampering and coddling her along with the others. Even she had been against Rory's plans to join her brother, though she had neither the desire nor the authority to stop her. It was Doris who had also suggested she bring some kind of older, more comfortable shoes and who had surreptitiously tucked her sneakers in at the bottom of her suitcase, though

Rory herself had claimed her new cowboy boots were as comfortable as any walking shoes. Now, having seen the way she had faltered over the gravel at this last stop, she had to agree with Doris. It was very probable once she was at the site, that she would have to sacrifice several extra inches of vanity for comfort and, indeed, safety.

The tall stranger had known it too; her clothes were not only out of place here but could well prove to be impractical. Warmth, for one thing, might be a problem, she pondered as she turned up the heat of the jeep. The sun had cast a certain warmth to morning back in Whitehorse, but now it was blocked by heavy clouds more often than not, and the steady gain in altitude as she proceeded north did nothing to take the chill from her feet.

The tall stranger . . . her mind couldn't help but muse about him. Where was he now? Where had he come from? Where was he going? Who was he? Was it only the monotony of the drive that had brought him to mind? No, she chided herself, her thoughts had turned to him, as they had done intermittently all night, with no connection to the monotony ahead or behind. The man was an enigma. She knew nothing about him—nothing, except that he had the power to infuriate her with his frankness, as he had mesmerized her with his kiss.

The latter was an awesome power, indeed. For Rory had always considered herself to be one of the few of her species left: the old-time, prim and proper, dyed-in-the-wool virgins—though less because of high moral standards than pure and simple physical distaste. She constantly dated the most available and willing partners, each of whom was in his turn sent to the showers, often rudely humiliated by an outraged and uncaring Rory. Indeed, her reputation as an untouchable had begun to precede her, eliminating those suitors with only fun and games on the mind, while doing nothing to discourage those obsessed with dreams of wealth. Rory had never been particularly bothered by the image, as there had never been anyone who had begun to excite her. Even with Charles, the attraction had been intellectual, never physical. No, no one had remotely excited her in that most primitive way. Until now.

The tall stranger . . . who was he? The question haunted her relentlessly as she drove on beneath an increasingly overcast and ominous sky. His kiss . . . so firm yet tentative, evoking a response she had doubted she possessed. *Who was he?*

Her thoughts were broken by the first large raindrops, which the gusting wind quickly blew from the windshield. Soon they were coming faster and closer together, until the glass was blurred by long streaks, and Rory was forced to turn on the wipers. Before long, it had turned into a full-fledged downpour. Slowing to a snail's pace on the slick gravel, Rory fought to stay calm as she struggled to keep sight of the road, suddenly inundated with puddles. Her headlights had been on all along, as was the rule on gravel roads according to the signs, yet the light did nothing to improve the visibility.

Among the many differing emotions her present situation evoked, Rory was most acutely aware of the feeling of aloneness, of being totally on her own to face nature's fury. Well, she reasoned, she had wanted to emerge from the cocoon, hadn't she? There was certainly no guardian here, she realized, as the jeep hit a puddle and plowed through, spewing water to either side.

Suddenly, a maelstrom of doubts engulfed her. Perhaps Daniel had been right. Should she turn around and return to Whitehorse? No, she had come too far. Or had she? How much farther did she have to go? Daniel had talked of anywhere from five to fifteen hours. Was he being facetious about the latter? She must certainly have come a third of the way. No, there would be no turning back, she resolved. Slowly and carefully, she would push forward.

Just then, a dark blur caught her eye. Slowly the blur moved closer, taking shape as it did so, until she made out a motorcycle and its rider, hailing her from the shoulder of the road. It had been rule number two, right after never to accept candy from strangers: Never stop for a hitchhiker! This situation was surely different, though. First, it would seem to be no more than common decency on a deserted highway like this to aid a fellow traveler in distress. Second, it was actually a relief to see someone, anyone, in the midst of the torrent. Third, there was a definite familiarity in the form of this hitchhiker, from the high boots, to the tall slimness, to the confident stance, to the touch of red wool peeking from a back pocket. The first two arguments she could feasibly have ignored; the third she could not. There was something about the stranger she'd met yesterday, and if this were indeed he . . .

With a grinding halt amid the muck of the gravel, she pulled the jeep over to the side just ahead of the rider, then turned in her seat to wait while he ran to the passenger door, opened it, tossed a bundle into the back, and slid out of the rain onto the seat beside her. Rain dripped from the helmet he removed as he spoke, looking over at her only after the helmet had been tossed onto the floor mat. "Much obli— Well, if it isn't . . ."

The moment of recognition was mutual, for Rory the realization of what she had already envisioned. Rain-drenched features notwithstanding, the amber eyes, straight nose, and well-formed lips amid a trimmed black beard left no doubt as to the identity of this hitchhiker.

"Rory Matthews!" he exclaimed with a sly grin, doubtlessly pleased by her state of momentary speechlessness. "Rory Matthews," he repeated, deliberately reminding her of his opinion of her name, even as he chided her, "you should be ashamed of yourself!"

Her eyes rounded as she stared at him in confusion. "What?"

"You should be ashamed of yourself . . . stopping for a hitchhiker! First you provoke a poor man in a bar, now you do something as irresponsible as—"

"I don't believe you!" she broke in. "We are in the midst of a torrential downpour, I spot a familiar face stranded by the wayside—stupid enough to have been on a motorcycle, I might add—I stop to offer him a lift, and you call that irresponsible?" Her eyes flashed dangerously. "Okay, get out! Now!" Furiously and futilely she pushed at the granite arm and shoulder nearest her, when she suddenly found both wrists imprisoned in the steel vise of one of her victim's hands.

"Take it easy, girl. No offense intended." His action had stilled her, and he easily released her wrists as soon as he felt her resistance end. "My, but you're touchy," he commented as she drew her hands back to the steering wheel. Perhaps it had been the pent-up tension of her early-morning escape, then this frightening turn of the weather; perhaps it had been his accusation, one more voice suggesting she'd never make it on her own; perhaps it was merely *him,* and the most disturbing effect he had on her. Whatever, she forced herself to calm down.

"You could thank me for stopping," she began, her words popping out automatically, the attitude of superiority one of habit and a far cry from the words of apology, which would have been more appropriate.

Bullheadedness was apparently not one of his traits. "Thank you. It was kind." He smiled solicitously, a mischievous twinkle rippling the smooth amber pools.

Not to be appeased so easily, Rory snapped tartly, "Don't patronize me," then, remembering herself, she continued more patiently. "Where are you going?"

"Into the Selwyn range."

"On a cycle?" Now it was she who reproved.

He challenged amiably, "And why not?"

"Gravel roads, for one thing." She gestured to the mess around them. "Bad weather, for another."

He laughed in sudden comprehension. "And who tried to scare *you* off . . . that fellow back at the inn?"

Her retort came a little too quickly. "*I'm* not on a motorcycle. And no one tried to scare me off. He simply . . . discouraged me from going. . . ." She couldn't hide, nor did she try to ignore, the anger that the memory of Daniel's words revived.

"A lover's spat?" His eyes impaled her as she realized, for the first time, the conclusion he had reached back at the inn. Far be it for her to disillusion him, she decided impulsively.

"I wouldn't say that," she replied evasively, doing nothing to correct the obvious misunderstanding. Just then, their attention was diverted by a truck traveling in the opposite direction. To Rory's surprise, it slowed and came to a stop just beside her door. Rolling down her window a bit, she barely managed to catch the driver's words through the din of the storm.

"You folks all right?"

She smiled and nodded, as much of a response as the fellow needed to send him on his way once again. Rolling her window back up to stop the driving rain from pouring into the jeep, Rory realized that she was again alone with—and at the mercy of—this compelling stranger. And her first instinct was to remedy a situation which had bothered her since yesterday. "What is your name?" she asked shyly, at once surprised by her tone of timidity.

He smiled broadly, white teeth sparkling and rain-drops still glistening on his beard. "I was wondering when you would ask. Eric Clarkson, at your service. Er, or is it the other way around?" He laughed again, amazing Rory with his spirit in the midst of such discouraging elements. "It seems that I am at *your* mercy." Funny, she thought, how she had assumed him to have the upper hand. "Where are *you* headed?" he asked.

"Through Ross River," she answered, purposely being vague, though in truth unable to be much more specific. The man, actually, did not seem to be dangerous, she acknowledged, except in terms of the power he held over her. It puzzled her that she reacted so differently to him than she had to others. In his presence the annoyance, the indifference, the pomposity, the imperiousness were all forced. She liked him, she realized, though she wasn't at all sure why.

"Don't you think we should be going, then?" he broke into her thoughts. "That is, you don't mind if I ride with you, do you?" He was teasing her, knowing full well the answer to his question.

In fact, the only answer was the sound of the

engine turning over, then revving up as she shifted into gear, and they were on their way. The rain had continued its angry pace, and now, as Rory drove on slowly, the wipers pounding at their fastest speed yet doing little to clear the windshield, the road showed the effects. It was fury upon fury; this hard land, which battered the human form at every turn, now being itself battered by an even greater force.

"Shall I drive?" he offered quietly, noting the white-knuckled hands which held on to the steering wheel for dear life.

Her voice betrayed her tension. "No. I can handle it!" She was used to the jouncing; the makeshift cushion had helped. She was even beginning to decipher patterns through the spatter and blotch on the windshield. It was mostly a matter of color distinction, the charcoal-grays of the gravel contrasting with the charcoal-green of the trees. She gave her total concentration to her chore, ignoring leg muscles that threatened to cramp under the tension. Conversation was out of the question, so demanding was the driving. She did spare a moment, however, for smug satisfaction over how well she was doing.

Unfortunately, her self-congratulation was premature. From far down the road her greatest fear materialized in the form of a large truck, advancing upon them at a reckless pace. Rory braced herself for the onslaught, but was nonetheless unprepared for what happened. As the truck rushed past, without slackening its speed in the slightest, a hail of water and gravel, mud and debris hit the windshield with such force that she was temporarily blinded and terrified that she might lose control.

"You're doing fine. Just hold it straight," her passenger ordered, calmly yet firmly, as the truck

passed and the deluge slackened, leaving her badly
shaken and frankly amazed that she had been able to
avoid a potential calamity. Knowing that she needed
at least a moment to recover, she pulled to the side
of the road and stopped, breathing deeply as she
rested her head on the steering wheel. For all practical purposes, she was oblivious to the man beside
her, until his voice reminded her of his presence.

"Let me drive for a while," he suggested, with a
thoughtfulness that referred to the heavy tension of
driving in the storm rather than to any inability on
her part. Raising her still-pale face to his, Rory saw a
genuine concern in his expression, and she nodded,
only too happy to yield the wheel.

Moving forward in his seat, he gently took her arm
and slid her sideways, sweaters and all, flipping himself over and behind the wheel with no hesitancy, a
remarkable feat for a man of his size. "All set?" Again,
she nodded, taking a deep breath to still the racing of
her heartbeat. As the jeep moved back onto the road,
he surprised her by offering his compliments. "You
handle the jeep very well. Are you used to driving
one?"

His eyes were glued to the blurred image ahead;
this necessity enabled her now to look him over
leisurely, even as she gave him an evasive, though
basically honest response to his inquiry. "I was
weaned on a stick and clutch. Aside from size and
style, this isn't much different from my own car." His
profile was, she decided, as powerful as his full face,
the straight line of his nose suggesting a patrician
fineness, which his chin, had it been visible beneath
the beard, would no doubt have reinforced. His
hands were strong on the steering wheel, though far
from tense, as hers had been. His outfit fascinated

her, a blend of the preppy and the biker: soaked leather jacket, open now to reveal a shetland sweater, equally wet denims, clinging to his well-muscled thighs, and high-quality boots. There was a strange richness about him, both in his dress and in his manner. Rory found her curiosity rising. "You left your bike behind," she ventured. "Aren't you worried about it?"

He looked quickly over at her, catching the way she had her knees tucked up under her for warmth before his attention riveted back to the road. Without a word, he reached forward and raised the heat another notch. "It's just a machine. I'll have it picked up later. When it becomes a thing of danger, it's as well left behind. Here,"—he paused, extending one arm toward her—"give me a hand with this, will you?" Instinctively, she reached over and helped him remove the sodden jacket, rising to her knees to ease it off. Inadvertently, as the jeep jolted along, her breast touched his near shoulder, sending a deep and unfathomable current through her. "Thank you," he murmured softly, his tone reminiscent of what had followed their kiss. His amber gaze had a wicked gleam to it, though its immediate return to the stormy path ahead mercifully relieved her of any undue embarrassment.

And the storm around them raged on unabated, though Rory felt strangely relaxed now that this man had taken over the responsibility of driving. Eric Clarkson. Well, she mused, he did have a name, as well as a great face and body, or so she surmised from the way his clothes molded it. And he had a flair for adventure, if the motorcycle was any indication of his tastes. Already, he had one up on most of the men she had hitherto known!

"You said you were on vacation. What do you normally do?" Her eyes rested on the uncallused hands.

"I'm in business."

"That says a lot," she murmured sarcastically, half to herself and half aloud. "What sort of business?"

He glanced over at her curly head, cocked in curiosity, her green eyes now warm and luminous. He couldn't help but linger to admire her luxuriant lashes, only reluctantly drawing his eyes back to the road—just in time to see the dark form enter the road but yards ahead.

"Hold on," he ordered suddenly, his right arm flinging across her middle as he slammed on the brakes. Rory had no time to catch her breath as the jeep skidded on the gravel, fishtailing to the right then the left before turning into a shallow gully beyond its shoulder. Trembling with shock, she held on to the arm that supported her, absorbing its strength as the outside world stopped spinning and the engine died, leaving only the sound of pounding rain in chorus with two wildly beating hearts.

She didn't realize how ragged her breathing was until a firm hand took her chin and turned it toward him. "Are you all right, Rory?" Numbly, she nodded, aware only of how grateful she was for his concern.

"What happened?" she whispered breathlessly.

As he reached back to put on his jacket he was suddenly impatient. "A moose crossing the road. If I hadn't been distracted"—he shot her an annoyed look—"I might have seen it sooner. Now I think we may have damaged a wheel. Stay here." Before she could protest, he had opened the door and disappeared into the rain, leaving Rory to feel guilty and perplexed. It seemed like an eternity before he returned, soaked and angry.

"Well?" She prodded, anxious to know the extent of the damage to the vehicle, which she suddenly realized was her own responsibility.

"Flat tire, that's all," he mumbled, as he turned to glare at her through dripping lashes.

Rory was taken aback by his expression. "What are you angry at me for?" she accused, bewildered. "It's not my fault! You were the one who was driving. And what's so difficult about changing a tire?"

"Are *you* planning to change it?" he retorted, his manner easing ironically as her own temper flared.

She laughed incredulously. "I have no intention of changing any tire when I've got someone as big and strong as you are to do it for me." Then realizing what she had said and how she had said it, a sudden shame swept over her, and she hastened to rescue her fast-fleeing new image. "Never mind," she murmured softly, looking away from his piercing gaze, "I'll try—"

"You'll do no such thing!" His abrupt about-face took her by surprise and she looked back at him questioningly. "Rory, it's impossible to do anything until this rain ends. The tire is in mud up to its axle. A jack would not begin to raise the thing." His eyes studied her frown, then twinkled lightly. "I guess you're stuck with me for a while."

"She looked at him with sudden alarm at her own vulnerability. "What do you mean?"

"Well," he began softly, "we have a choice. Either we wait here for the weather to clear or another vehicle to pass and see us, or we look around for some tracks leading off into the woods. The way I see it, we won't be able to budge this jeep—"

"Tracks leading off into the woods?" She gasped in horror, the weight of their predicament settling in on her. "What tracks? Leading where?"

He shrugged as he reached into an inner pocket of his jacket and withdrew a map. "I'm not quite as foolhardy as you suspect, my dear." His calm, near-humorous drawl turned her horror to astonishment. "Any _responsible_ person would know, on a road like this, of the existence and location of shelter, in case of just this type of emergency." The map held his full attention for several moments before he looked up. "When I stopped the bike, I figured I might have to walk to this point." A long, bronzed finger pointed to a notation on the map. "It would have been a mighty long walk, I'm afraid. If my calculations are correct, however, your jeep has delivered us practically to the front door." His gaze penetrated the windshield in search of the specific landmark.

"The front door?" Her voice was a blend of doubt and out-and-out incredulity.

The dark head nodded slowly, amber eyes never leaving the roadside. "It's a good guess that there's a cabin not too far off. It is most likely deserted, but could mean a dry, maybe even warm shelter until things dry off a bit." His eyes narrowed. "According to the map, there should be a birch cluster on either side of the path. Everything is so dim, though, in this—wait!" His facial muscles relaxed and Rory followed the line of his eyes. "That's it. Up the road, over there to the right."

Sure enough, two birch clusters could be deciphered in the distance, barely visible against the green-black foliage. Unable to share Eric's relief, Rory was besieged by doubts, not the least of which had to be the prospect of spending time in a secluded and deserted cabin with this commanding personality beside her.

"That's just great," she muttered in desperation,

her otherwise soft pink lips tightly drawn in dismay. What really was her choice? The jeep and its contents were her responsibility. She couldn't very well desert it by hitching a ride on a passing vehicle (perish the thought!), nor could the two of them just sit there, cramped and chilly, for endless hours. Maybe there *was* a cabin nearby. Could Eric be right? Peering out the window, she could see so little.

"These tracks," she began slowly, none too sure of herself. "Perhaps we'd better check them out. We can't very well stay here." Hesitantly, she glanced at Eric, wondering what his reaction would be to her suggestion. To her astonishment, his face lit up immediately.

"Atta girl! You wait here while I explore—"

"No way!" she interrupted, regaining spirit instantly. "I can explore just as well as you can and that way, if there *is* a cabin, we'll be there sooner." Her extremities were already colder than she dared to admit, and she suspected that she might be more frightened sitting alone and wondering whether he would make it back.

"Sure you can make it?"

"Of course," she snapped, willing herself to rise to the occasion. She was no longer to be pampered!

"Okay." He shrugged, accepting her decision as final. "Now let's bring whatever we can carry, keep dry, and make ourselves useful. Have you any rain gear?" She shook her head. "Sleeping bag?" Again, the negative shake. These things, as well as other supplies, she'd had every intention of picking up that morning, under Daniel's tutelage—had he only been agreeable to her intentions. Her premature flight had left her pathetically ill prepared. "Flashlight?" he asked, his tone becoming accusatory. About to respond as she had done twice now, she suddenly remembered the glove compartment, from which she quickly and triumphantly extracted a large and fairly strong searchlight. "Good." He smiled her instant redemption. "How about food?"

Her head shook once more, an apologetic expression on her face, until she remembered the supplies Daniel had picked up and her eyes lit up. "I think there may be something back here," she exclaimed, as she turned and leaned over the back of the seat to examine the boxes piled high behind.

He stared at her in dismay. "You *think?* Don't you even know what you've got here? Or did you highjack the lot?"

"*Now* you understand," she quipped. He should only know the truth, she mused slyly. "Can you give me a hand?" She tumbled nimbly into the backseat, a solid shove to her backside speeding up her trip. Only when she regained her balance did she turn and glare at him. "That wasn't exactly what I had in mind."

The light in his eyes flashed also, but with an emotion which took Rory off guard. "Then from now on, you'd better specify what you have in mind, little one," he drawled suggestively.

"*You'd* better watch it, bud," she warned imperiously, infuriated more by the appellation he'd chosen than by his action. The tone had always worked before. . . .

"Or what?" he challenged, his eyelids lowering much too seductively for her peace of mind.

She paused, studying him, as she chose to ignore his bait. "You're really enjoying this, aren't you?" she accused wryly.

His look miraculously became one of supreme

innocence. "Enjoying what? Your company or the storm?"

"This . . . this whole thing," she stammered furiously, throwing her hands up in exasperation. "You enjoy tormenting me. You did it yesterday, you're doing it now. You see this as a great adventure, don't you? And you'll get your amusement at my expense, is that it?"

He opened his mouth to comment on her claim, when she quickly continued. "Well, don't plan on it." She spoke through clenched teeth. "I was good enough to stop for you. That was my first mistake. I even let you drive. That was my second mistake. But I'm now through making mistakes. Got it?" Her speech was no more acid than many a one she had delivered to unsuspecting and ofttimes undeserving beaux, yet she regretted her tone as soon as she heard herself, sounding more spoiled and pompous than was justified.

Thus embarrassed by her words for not the first time in this man's company, she set to work hastily searching through the cartons for food. The silence within the car was heavy, despite the loud pounding of the storm against the roof of the jeep. She dared not look up, sensing correctly that sharp amber eyes would tear into her if she did so. What she did not expect was the opening of the door as he climbed out, followed quickly by its forceful slam. By the time she lifted her eyes to the soggy landscape, there was no sign of him. Had her words been correct, she should have breathed a sigh of relief; yet it was more a gasp of apprehension that escaped her lips as she sought to remain levelheaded.

Despite his occasional lapses, he had struck her as being a responsible person. Surely he wouldn't desert her, she reasoned. Yet, she couldn't just sit here and wait, like a lost child, until he decided to fetch her. No, she had assured him that she could follow those tracks as well as he could, and that, she told herself determinedly, was precisely what she would do.

Digging further into the boxes, she reached several cases of canned goods, grabbing an armful and wrapping them, along with the flashlight, carefully within the heaviest of her sweaters. As luck would have it, she discovered a large piece of plastic around one of the pieces of glaciological equipment, and this she wrapped in turn around the sweater, throwing in her pocketbook for good measure. Not knowing how far she would be walking, she didn't venture to carry anything else. Carefully, she climbed into the front seat, opened the door, and slid out, locking the door behind her—though she doubted whether any living soul would even see the vehicle, much less loot it, in this weather.

The rain steadily pelted her as she timidly moved forward in search of the tracks Eric had referred to. Sure enough, a bit ahead and to the right, a double set of tracks, more like parallel puddles, extended into the woods. The prospect of what she was about to do terrified her, and for a moment, Rory toyed with the idea of returning to the jeep to meekly await rescue. That was exactly what the Rory back home would have done and without doubt would have been promptly rescued. But this Rory was not back home, and Eric Clarkson was not quite the pushovers who had always surrounded her.

With this resolve, she slowly began to follow the tracks, keeping to the high ground as much as possible. At best the soil was soft and wet; at worst it was little better than quicksand. The trees at least seemed to form an umbrella of sorts, dulling the force of the rain. All else, however, seemed against her. The farther she progressed, the darker it grew, though her watch showed little past midday. She couldn't imagine the storm worsening, though from the din above her she momentarily imagined hailstones joining the raindrops.

By this time, her boots were soaked through. Her clothes too were quickly becoming saturated, though she guessed they would dry satisfactorily if there was, indeed, a cabin and some warmth ahead. Fortunately the pack she carried remained dry. She paused occasionally to push a dripping strand of hair back, as she strained her eyes to see some sign of life.

A noise startled her from behind, and she whirled around to see the tail end of an animal, small and dark and furry, disappear into the bushes. Up to that point, she had given no thought to the wildlife she might encounter, and she nearly panicked. After all, a moose had been the original cause of this fiasco; what other creatures might there be? Temporarily paralyzed with fear, she again found herself wondering whether to go forward or backward. Had she come too far to turn around? Once more her decision was to move on, now keeping an eye to either side as well as ahead and underfoot, with the occasional glance behind for good measure.

Chilled to the bone, Rory felt as though she'd been tramping through the woods for an hour when in fact it had been no more than ten minutes. She was about to turn back when the smell of burning wood drifted toward her. It was easy to guess the source of this smoke. An unknown resource gave her the strength to rush forward in its direction, leading her quickly to a clearing at the center of which stood an old and rather decrepit-looking cabin, its windows boarded up, its door hanging none too steadily on rusted hinges, but its erect albeit precariously tilted chimney sending the precious smoke signals to lead her in.

She ran the last distance, unmindful of the mud, her sole desire being to escape the down-pour, to dry off, to warm up. The door yielded easily, admitting her to a very dark, very primitive, but mercifully dry and warm room. At the far side, was the source of the smoke, a fireplace, where a healthy fire was being nursed by the tall, lean figure she had known would be there.

Eric made no acknowledgment of her arrival, merely continued to prod the fire with a bent poker of sorts. Although she hadn't expected a welcoming committee, Rory, frankly pleased at having reached the cabin on her own, was disappointed that he did not grant the praise she felt was due. But then, she chided herself impatiently, what she'd just done, a milestone for her, was nothing more than millions of people did many times during their lives. She had merely taken one more step toward joining the rest of the human race!

Accepting the fact that no congratulations would be forthcoming, she plopped her plastic package down beside her as she quickly moved close to the fire. Eric had moved to one side of the room, rummaging through something about which she neither knew nor cared. Her first concern was to dry off. And this she did, peeling her soaking clothes from her body without delay and letting the glow of the fire dry her bare skin as she spilled out the contents of the package, reached for her sweater, and drew it over her damp head, unconsciously combing her hair with her fingers. It was a seductive move of which she was totally ignorant. In retrospect, she was to marvel at her lack of concern for Eric during this immodest change of clothes; at the time she thought nothing of it, being so accustomed to do what she wanted when she wanted that nothing seemed amiss, until long denim legs and bare feet came between her and the fire.

"That was mistake number three." The low voice startled her with a huskiness she had not heard before. "Never undress like that in front of a man, unless you intend it as an invitation." He knelt down until his eyes met hers. "Despite your low opinion of me, I am a man, with the needs and desires to prove it."

Rory stared at him speechlessly. A gentle hand on each of her shoulders drew her up until her face was but inches from his. Lacking the will, any will, to pull back, she gazed at him, mesmerized, as the amber eyes caressed her, touching each feature: her green orbs, wide with wonder, her faintly flushed cheeks, the delicate line of her nose, and her soft lips, now parted and faintly quivering. It was excruciatingly sweet torture as he slowly bridged the gap and his lips touched hers, finally and exquisitely, tasting, probing, then devouring with a fierceness born of unabashed desire, crushing her body against the tautness of his with an all-consuming need.

For Rory, the spell was powerful, as reality receded and the senses reigned victorious. She felt his tongue against her teeth, exploring and teasing recesses she willingly offered, as her own tongue became an active player in the erotic scenario. It was as though he held the key, that very special key, which unlocked all of the wonders of womanhood previously withheld from her.

Instinctively, her hands moved against his arms and over his shoulders, reveling in the strength of the muscles rippling beneath his sweater before intertwining themselves in the smooth hair at the nape of his neck. Her muscles, every nerve end, came alive under his exploration. She trembled as large hands moved beneath the looseness of her sweater and over the smooth skin of her back, tracing her spine to its base, then moving sideways along her hips. Her gasp was one of surprise, not so much at what he touched, as at what his touch did to her, to that inexplicable tightening at her stomach's pit.

And all the while, his lips played on hers, balancing the fierceness with a tenderness she could not have imagined possible. Now, slowly, they searched a path to her throat, drawing from her lips a sigh at the sensual beauty of his touch.

"*Was* it an invitation?" he drawled huskily, as he raised his head to gaze into her eyes.

She was too overcome with emotion to respond, thrilled by the strength of his body so close to hers, devastated by the withdrawal of his firm lips, confounded by the throbbing deep within her. Under the weight of her burden, her eyes filled with tears as she shook her head. "No," she whispered, though the words were merely mouthed, as a knot in her throat prevented all sound.

"Then I suggest you be more careful in the future," he murmured impatiently, yet pausing to kiss away the tears at her eyelids, their salt a welcome sting on his burning lips. "I'm not sure how strong I can continue to be." Abruptly, he drew her hands from his neck and moved away. Stunned and bereft, Rory sat back on her heels for a moment, unable to function until his note of annoyance brought her the rest of the way back to reality. "Rory . . ." His voice trailed off, its threat undisguised as his gaze fell to her bare legs.

Pants . . . she looked around, realizing that her wet denims were the only things that would fall into this category. Reaching for them, she was once again startled.

"On second thought," the deep voice charged, "they're wet. Why don't you let them dry a bit before the fire."

"But you just said—" she began, eyeing him warily.

"And I've just changed my mind. That sweater will do the trick, as long as you keep it *on*," he explained. "You look almost childlike in it, definitely not the seductress type."

She glared at him, infuriated that he had destroyed the beauty of the moment with such hurtful banter. "You . . . you oaf!" She scowled, impulsively grabbing her jeans and struggling to pull them on, a none too simple feat, considering their sodden condition.

Out of the corner of her eye, she caught his approach. "Here, let me give you a hand. It's the least—"

"Leave me alone!" she shrieked, pulling frantically at the pants leg he had grabbed, her own leg thus a prisoner of both her jeans and his hand. Kicking at him angrily, she lost her balance, falling unceremoniously onto the dirt floor. To her dismay, her companion followed her down, the weight of his body pinioning her to the floor, his hands spread-eagling hers above her head.

"You really are a delight." He laughed playfully, as he placed a quick kiss on her lips and then bounded up. He stood above her for a moment longer, savoring his coup, before he added, "Very refreshing," as he turned to walk away.

Unable to resist, Rory drew her unencumbered leg off to one side, then swung it with all her force at his shin, yelling out in pain as her toes made contact with iron. "Aach! What have you got down there . . . steel plates?"

He laughed heartily, in obvious enjoyment of her self-inflicted punishment, as he quipped, "Maybe someday I'll show you . . . when you've grown up a little." And he walked to the other side of the room to give his attention to something more pressing.

three

HIS COMMENT HAD HURT MUCH MORE THAN an injured toe ever could have. Carefully, Rory eased the other leg of her jeans, now both wet and dirty from the grime of the cabin floor, over the tender toe and painstakingly pulled the pants up, rising unsteadily to zip and snap them. Thus adequately dressed, she turned her full attention to the warmth of the fire.

Only part of her attention was on it, however. The other part dwelt on what had happened so freely and spontaneously moments ago. She knew so little about this Eric Clarkson, yet she felt so drawn to him. He looked to be in his midthirties, a far cry from her tender twenty-one, though she had indeed dated men his age and older. He looked clean-cut, beard and all, he spoke and acted well bred, motorcycle and sexual prowess notwithstanding, and he found her physically attractive, wisecracks about her age and maturity to the contrary.

Yet he was an independent sort, she knew instinctively. He would have no woman dictate to him, as

she had always done to the men in her life—yes,
even as she had tried so unsuccessfully to do just
before he had abandoned her at the jeep. Although
he had given her the impression, back there, that the
decision about what to do was hers, she suspected
that he would have promptly overturned it had he
not already decided on the very same himself.

Was it this independence that excited her so? Or
was it something deeper? She had never ever been as
turned on by any man's touch. Its power frightened
her, not the least of which fright were the new and
unexpected reactions within her own body. It
occurred to her that here in this dilapidated log
cabin, in a never-neverland of sorts, she could lose
herself completely to this man's sensual appeal.
Apprehensively, she looked over in his direction, to
see him struggling with one of the cans she had toted
from the jeep. A can opener . . . how foolish . . . did
he have one?

Impulsively, she jumped up and approached him,
limping only slightly as her toes returned to normal.
He was indeed trying to open the can, though with a
metal object that looked neither strong enough nor
sharp enough to do the trick.

"I have a nail clipper in my bag. Will that help?"
she inquired timidly, her voice sounding strange
even to her.

He looked up, smirking as he took in the warmed,
though still very damp, denims. "It's worth a try!"
Quickly she turned, retrieved her pocketbook, and
rummaged through its contents until her hand
closed on the small sharp object. She held it out
toward him, his hand immediately closing on it and
squeezing her own simultaneously, in a subtle gesture of appreciation. "Thanks," he murmured softly,

as he offered her a broad grin. Rory could have asked no greater reward for her ingenuity than that one, sparkling smile.

"Got it," he exclaimed triumphantly several moments later, as the top of the can was folded back to reveal a glob of corned beef hash, far from gourmet fare, but nourishing. "Let's see what else you've got," he suggested, going over to the plastic wrapping and spilling its remaining contents on the ground. "Hmmm, not bad. Mixed vegetables, sweet potatoes, sloppy joes. Not bad at all. I may go back and get some more before it gets dark."

Rory eyed him incredulously. "Just how many meals do you expect to eat here?"

Undaunted, he explained calmly, "I haven't had anything to eat since last night, and a poor excuse for a dinner *that* was! Not that I would have noticed what I was eating anyway. . . ." His voice trailed off, the implication of his words unclear to her, as his mind wandered on some unfathomable subject; then he resumed his reasoning. "I'm famished now. That still leaves supper and breakfast—"

"Hold it!" she interrupted. "You talk as though the only thing you have to do here is to eat!"

He eyed her through lowered lids. "And what else did *you* have in mind, Rory?"

"Oh, stop it!" She looked away in embarrassment, marveling at the limited track of the man's mind. "I don't know . . . watch the fire, count the raindrops . . ." She was only getting herself in deeper, she feared. "And anyway, those supplies don't belong to me."

"Ah, that's right." He humored her with a devilish smile. "But if you expect me to change that tire, I'll have to be well fed."

"That's blackmail!" she accused, knowing that he

could have as much of the food as he wanted, if she had to pay Daniel back herself. Reluctant to concede defeat, she turned and paced back to the fire as another thought occurred to her. "But it's a long way back to the jeep and the ground is getting no drier," she argued.

A boisterous laugh met her protestation. "It's not that far. It took me less than five minutes to get here before, although it did take you considerably longer. But you made it. I was proud of you. I bet you haven't done this type of thing before, have you?" He had approached the fire himself, squatting down beside her as he talked.

Now it was Rory's turn to snicker. "Not by a long shot. I was always too afraid that my clothes would get dirty!" Her ability to laugh at herself, for a change, was refreshing.

"Where do you come from?" he asked gently.

"Seattle. All my life." She gazed into the fire, remembering the beautiful colonial masterpiece, built on a prime piece of wooded land on the outskirts of the city. As a child, she had viewed it as a palace, her parents the king and queen, her brother and she the royal prince and princess. The world had been so simple then, full of warmth and happiness and every imaginable goody that a young child could desire. Then, one day, the bubble popped and the dream world crumbled, as the father, whom she had wholeheartedly adored, disappeared from the kingdom, leaving the queen and her retinue to reign as he established his new throne elsewhere. It had been a blow perhaps more to Rory than to anyone else. She was too young to understand, too old to forget easily. In an act of self-preservation, she turned to her mother, then increasingly to her brother, for the attention that had been so rudely and abruptly denied her.

"Are the memories that painful?" He prodded softly, intently studying her expression, which betrayed her thoughts.

Her gaze jerked to his, embarrassed by her own transparency. "You see too much," she murmured, quickly looking back at the fire as if she could thereby hide her feelings. At this point in her life, her past was what she wanted to escape.

Eric did not give up so easily. "Do you have family there?"

"Now?" she asked, catching his subtle nod. "No." It was the literal truth, no more, no less. "I thought you were hungry," she reminded him, his questions hitting closer to home than she wanted.

He eyed her thoughtfully for a moment before deciding to let her off the hook. Then he smiled, that warm and dazzling smile, which removed the inner chill as no fire ever could. "Hmmm, you're right. I had almost forgotten. I guess there *is* more to life than food." He rose to retrieve several cans.

Rory watched him go, his every movement in fluid harmony with its predecessor. He carried himself like the ultimate athlete, his body trained not to waste an ounce of vital energy. Once again he was by her side, laying out the menu in a neat row. Although she might have been tempted, had the fare been, say, canned sardines, or even tuna, the look of the corned beef hash convinced her to save her appetite for dinner.

"Won't you join me?" he asked, humor written all over his face and indicating that, once more, he had read her sentiments.

She swallowed hard before she answered. "Thank you, but I think I'll wait." Then, several thoughts occurred to her. "Hey, how are you going to cook it . . . or eat it, for that matter?"

The look of lingering amusement was now accentuated by an easy laugh. "You never were a Girl Scout, were you?"

Emitting a sigh of mock resignation, she shook her head. "None of the mothers in my neighborhood were willing to be leaders." It may have been the case, for all she knew, though none of the girls would have even asked their mothers in the first place. Not in her neighborhood!

"Then you'll just have to call on that same resourcefulness you used to open the cans," he informed her cheerfully.

Impulsively, she reminded him, "But *you* opened the cans."

"Precisely. If we work together, your brains and my brawn, we may just make it!" Rory had to admire his confident grin, which precluded any doubt of his ability to "make it." It was her own ability that was in doubt here, she lamented.

Looking unsurely at him, she followed his gaze around the open room, taking in the rotted bed frame, whose legs may have been the kindling for the fire that roared robustly behind her, several broken chairs, and a wooden chest in a dark corner. Taking the flashlight, she approached it, Eric right beside her, as interested as she was. The metal lock and hinges had long since rusted, but fortunately they lay open. Eric reached forward to pry up the top, and the beam of the flashlight revealed a conglomeration of relics from the past. Yellowed and faded photographs of a wife or a mother, tattered letters, an old and infinitely worn Bible; all fascinating, though none particularly appropriate as cooking or eating utensils.

Except one. Gingerly reaching into the chest, Rory gasped with pleasure as she withdrew a round copper container nearly six inches in diameter. On its outside the most delicate dancing figures had been intricately carved. With growing excitement, she raised the lid, crying out with delight as it revealed itself to be a music box, tucked away thus for years, its song emerging in the most beautiful, yet mournful, melody Rory had ever heard.

"Isn't it exquisite?" she whispered breathlessly when the song had ended and so silently that her words were but a shadow of her thoughts.

"That's terrific!" Eric exclaimed, his enthusiasm startling her, its boisterousness totally incompatible with the object. "A copper pot," he went on gaily. "What more could we ask?"

She was puzzled, until she suddenly remembered his intention. "Oh, Eric, you wouldn't . . . it's so beautiful!" But her plea fell on deaf ears, as he took the music box from her hands and began to examine it closely to discover if he could take out its workings and convert it to more practical purposes.

"Please wait!" she begged. "Just let me listen again." Her soft green eyes seconded her plea, and with a short sigh, he handed it back to her. Winding it up as far as the key would turn, she listened, enraptured, as the melody repeated itself, simply and soulfully, bringing images of sadness and loneliness amid a strange beauty. As it played a final time, her mind recorded it, tracing indelible grooves upon her memory for all times. Then she silently handed it back to Eric, leaving him to his demolition while she returned to the fire.

There had been something special about the tune . . . or had it just been the time and place? As she gazed into the fire she wondered what others had wondered similarly in years gone by. The owner of the music box, the builder of this cabin . . . what others had passed this way, and had they found what they'd been seeking? That mournful melody, wordless and unrenowned, had spoken to Rory of a long road ahead. Was that what her own future held?

A sizzling sound distracted her, and the aroma of something—was it the hash or the vegetables, she wondered—wafted through the room. "That smells vile," she complained sharply to Eric, who was deftly maneuvering the copper pot between two lengths of pipe.

"Then it's a good thing you're not hungry." He removed the pot from the flames and set it down on the ground at the edge of the fire. "I'll be right back," he said, rising to go outside. "Don't eat my lunch while I'm gone," he cracked, then made a mad dash between the raindrops.

Moments later he returned, several thick pieces of curved bark in his hand. "Spoons," he announced proudly, settling himself cross-legged before the fire and proceeding, before Rory's astonished eyes, to down the gloppy mess. He glanced up at her appalled look, raising an eyebrow jauntily. "You'll never know what you're missing!"

"Thank God for small favors," she retorted, stretching herself out on her side before the fire. Suddenly, for some strange reason, she felt exhausted. Strange reason, my foot, she mused; she'd gotten practically no sleep the last night, had had a perfectly brutal—with several noteworthy exceptions—day, and had nothing better to do. Pulling over her pocketbook to serve as a pillow, she promptly drifted off into a deep sleep.

Images floated through her mind, some but fragmented bursts of thought, others more complete. Each in its turn faded away, relegated once more to the realm of the subconscious. Then, among the truncated visions, came a continuous one. It was a most terrifying scene, more accurately a void, filled with swirling masses of mist and fog through which she was frantically fleeing some unknown and unseen danger. She was aware only of the need to reach one of the far islands, vague and hazy, at an awesome distance from the steadily deteriorating patch of gloom which temporarily enswathed her. She could make out faces, one so very familiar and with a resemblance to her own, the other more strange yet more appealing. As she struggled for a foothold, moving forward bit by bit over an unearthly mesa, the faces only floated farther off, separating, moving closer, only to separate once more. She couldn't seem to gain any ground on them, merely groped and fumbled forward in vain. If only they would help her, if only she could reach them, either one of them. Panic-stricken, she called out her brother's name; surely he wouldn't let her drown in the swirling abyss. . . .

"Wake up, Rory." A firm hand shook her shoulder as an equally firm, almost angry voice mercifully rescued her. But the face she gazed at when she opened fearful eyes was not her brother's. This face was dark, the red glow of the fire casting a menacing light to its stern features.

"Eric." She sighed with relief as she pulled her quivering form up to a sitting position. "I had such an awful dream—"

"Spare me the details," he barked. "Here's some rope. I've just been back to the jeep to get more supplies." He was dripping wet; she should have guessed the reason.

"W-what time is it?" she asked, still trying to get her bearings and quiet her nerves, not the least bit helped by his sudden turn of temper.

"Almost six," he stated tersely, glaring angrily. "I want you to rig up this line somehow, so that we can hang the wet things on it. My sleeping bag is not too bad—"

"Sleeping bag? Where did you get a sleeping bag?"

"It's been with me all along," he retorted impatiently. "Didn't you see me bring it into the jeep when you first picked me up?" Meekly, she shook her head. No, she mused, she had been too taken by his physical presence at the time to notice anything else! "At least one of us knew what kind of equipment would be needed in the mountains!"

In another time, she would have argued against his unjustified claim; she had indeed known she'd need a sleeping bag, and would have bought one had she not had to escape so suddenly from Whitehorse. But then, Eric couldn't know that. And she was rendered silent by a new source of bewilderment: When, indeed, had she said she was going into the mountains?

"Here! Siesta time is over," he ordered, and dropped a pile of rope into her lap. Her eyes flew from the rope to his eyes, then back again. She had no idea of how to rig up a clothesline in this improbable setting, yet one final look into his threatening eyes told her that she'd have to find out.

Rising, she looked about, spotting a broken hinge on one of the windows and a group of nails directly opposite. Praying that the rope was long enough, she reached up to the hinge, straining on her tiptoes to tie one end around it, then slowly untangling the rope as she went, backed toward the other window, stopping no more than two feet short of her goal.

"Tsk, tsk. Try again." The low voice rubbed salt on the wound, though she noted with relief that some of the anger had been replaced by the mocking humor that was at least easier to bear. His anger was inexplicably cutting, and it bothered her that she should be so disturbed by it. After all, what did it matter if he hated her? By this time tomorrow they would have certainly parted ways, and she would never have to face him again.

"Well . . ." He prodded impatiently. "Am I going to have to wait forever?"

She turned to him, her bewilderment suddenly transformed into anger. "Oh, shut up! If you don't like the way I'm doing it, you can just do it yourself!" She had no more patience for his impatience than he had for her ineptitude.

Resuming the task, she moved toward a large iron hook embedded in the bricks of the fireplace; there the rope fit with several feet to spare. "Perfect," she muttered under her breath, as she climbed a pile of bricks to tie the rope, making sure that it was stretched taut. Then, emboldened by her success, she turned on her perch to confront her impassive audience. "I thought you were to supply the brawn for this operation. What's the matter? All tuckered out from that short walk in the woods?" she taunted, hands on hips.

"Not exactly," he responded, and before Rory could do anything to avoid him, he had scooped her up off her feet and into his arms.

She was acutely aware of his wet clothing against her side, the damp and musky smell of him. "Put me down!" she protested, pounding him with her hands and legs, but he only held her more firmly, as though to make his point.

"I'll let you go, little one, when I am good and ready. Don't ever forget that," he warned, releasing the hand beneath her knees, so that she slid into an upright position against him. As much as she wanted to fight him further, his nearness had begun to intoxicate her, and she could hear her heart thudding loudly against his chest.

"Now," he crooned seductively, "you have some work to do." Abruptly he released her, and it was by sheer chance that she kept her balance, wobbly as her knees had grown at his touch. He pointed to the place where she had carelessly dropped her drenched blouse and jacket. "Pick those up. There will be no maid service to clean up after you here! And I won't spend even one night in a pigsty!"

She stared at him, dumbfounded, but concluded that it would do her no good to argue. After all, he was bigger and stronger . . . and had just demonstrated that he would have his way. Obediently, if petulantly, she knelt to pick up the blouse and jacket, now filthy and still very wet. If they were going to hang to dry all night, they might as well be clean, she decided and moved around Eric to the door, feeling his eyes bore into her.

"Where do you think you're going?" he demanded.

She turned briefly to face him, her chin angled up defiantly. "These are dirty. If I'm going to wear them again, I'd like them to be clean. You see, I'm not quite the slob you seem to imagine."

"Oh, I never said you were a slob," he countered. His back was to the fire, his face in shadow, yet she could hear the grin in his words, and knew that he was more relaxed now and enjoying her discomfort. "I suspect, however, that you are used to being served by those around you."

Once again, Rory bristled. "And just what makes you think that?" Perhaps she'd temporarily begun to see herself as the capable woman Charles and Monica had inspired her to become; perhaps she'd merely hoped Eric might see her that way. Unfortunately, he did not.

"Come, come, Rory," he chided, sounding strangely like her older brother. "Everything about you reeks of the spoiled little girl—your tone, your words, your indignant glances, your haughtiness. And those lily-white hands." He lifted them in his, his thumbs caressing their backs as he continued, cocksure of himself, "So smooth and soft and positively allergic to manual labor."

Fighting a strange sensual urge, she snatched her hands from his and covered her unsureness with testiness. "What if I told you I wear rubber gloves when I do the dishes? Would you believe me?"

"No."

She glared at him. "Then that's your problem." She twirled to escape his burning amber gaze. Her movement was stilled by a firm hand on her arm.

"No, it's yours." His tone was matter-of-fact, and Rory believed every word he spoke. "I'm telling you that *I* won't serve you, that you'll have to pull your share of the weight."

"I have every intention of doing just that," she responded in a near whisper, a vow made as much for her own benefit as for his. Yet as Eric slowly released her arm, Rory could not help but rebel against his condescension. After all, it was her jeep: *she* had her upper hand. But it wasn't her jeep, she caught herself, any more than it was her upper hand, much as she might like to pretend so. Eric Clarkson intimidated her in a strange way, and while there was a perverse excitement in it, she doubted the wisdom of pushing him further than necessary.

It also astonished her that he should analyze her so correctly. As much as she was striving to change things, it was a fact that she *was* accustomed to being served, both emotionally and physically. Eric seemed to have a knack of seeing through her; she'd have to watch that!

"Here, give me a hand," he ordered, after she had rinsed her things off and hung them from the line. He unrolled his sleeping bag. "Flip this end over the line. I want the whole thing dry by night. It's getting cooler already." Rory took her end of the bag and threw it over the rope. Then she watched him stand his boots up by the fire and spread his jacket over the line. "Anything else that needs to dry?" he asked, eyeing her warily.

She looked around and shrugged. Her own boots were already by the fire, though she held little hope for their recovery, and her jeans had really done very well by the warmth of the fire as she had slept.

The sound of material drew her attention, and she looked over to see Eric pulling his damp shirt off, then hanging it beside his jacket. It was all she could do to keep from gasping audibly. There he stood, tall and lean before the fire, his chest bare to the wide belt above his hips. If she had any doubts about his strength before, she would no longer. His shoulders were bronzed and golden in the fire's glow, broad and muscled, his powerful arms framing a luxurious mat of dark, masculine chest hair that tapered to a thin line and vanished beneath his belt.

Had she been the Rory of days past, she would have boldly approached him, run her fingertips through his manly fur and along the line of well-shaped muscles. Why she should suddenly be overcome by shyness, she could not fathom. Grateful for the darkness, which hid her blush, she turned and opened the door to gaze out at the rain.

It was nearly dusk, an eerie bluish fog having settled over the woods, giving a surreal quality to the falling rain. The temperature seemed unusually chilly for summer, until she reminded herself how far north she'd come. As she stood there, a feeling of desolation engulfed her at the thought of being alone in the wilds, as she had been during her trek from jeep to cabin. Here, primitive and ill-equipped as the cabin was, she felt safe, warm, and dry. She shivered at the alternative.

"Come on back to the fire. I promise I won't attack you." Eric's voice was so soft and gentle, his hand at her shoulder so warm, that she could easily have burst into tears of frustration. As he slowly turned her around to face him, he saw the depth of emotion written so openly on her face. "What is it, little one?" he asked softly. Defensively, she shifted her eyes away from his face and toward his chest. A worse mistake she could not have made, as she was instantly gripped by yearnings, newborn yet all-powerful, to hold and be held, to touch and be touched.

He placed a strong finger beneath her chin, raising it to look into her eyes once again. "You're not afraid of me, are you?" She swallowed hard, shaking her head in a none too truthful denial. Her hands tingled, aching to feel his skin against her palms, yet she clenched them into fists, fighting for self-control. "Are you afraid of *him?*" he asked, his tone hardening.

Startled by his allusion, Rory knitted her brows in confusion. "Who?"

"I believe you called him Daniel when he so rudely interrupted us yesterday afternoon."

Funny, she had hardly thought of Daniel at all, yet her flight from him and the inevitability of having to face him soon should have kept him foremost in her mind. Not so, she realized, gazing at the one who was. "I wasn't thinking of Daniel. . . ." her voice trailed off, afraid to say more.

"But *are* you afraid of him?"

She nodded. "In a way you could say that." She adored her brother and regretted causing him so much trouble. Needless to say, he would contact his friends by radio, learn that she had not arrived, and be worried sick. Yes, she was afraid of his wrath, if the truth were told, though she knew it was merely a sign of his love for her, and she cherished that love.

Once again he lifted her face to his. "Come on. I won't make things harder. Let's get some supper going, then we'll talk." With that, he put one arm protectively across her shoulders, drawing her from the chill, pushed the door shut, and took her to the center of their present existence, the fire.

Sadly she pondered his words. "I won't make things harder," he had said. Oh, how much easier it was when he mocked her, berated her, ordered her around arrogantly. That was easy to resent. But warmth and understanding was an infinitely harder charm to resist. Yes, in that instant, Rory knew that Eric Clarkson was the most charming man she had ever met, not to mention the most handsome.

Mercifully, his attractiveness soon became easier to ignore when he settled himself in front of the fire and insisted that she prepare dinner. "It's your turn," he informed her.

"But I didn't get anything out of *your* turn," she protested, feeling much safer arguing with him.

"That was your choice. Come on, now. You must be starved!"

Truthfully, she was. It had been a long time since breakfast, and although she craved a cup of coffee above all else, she settled for the pork and beans that Eric produced from the supplies. With some difficulty, and to his thorough amusement, she noted wryly, she managed to heat the fare as he had done, running into trouble only when the pot had to be removed from the fire. It was a matter of balancing the thing between the two pieces of pipe, then transferring it to the ground.

Eric sat to the side while she struggled, neither an offer of help nor a practical suggestion forthcoming. Finally, tired, frustrated, and more than a little humiliated, she dragged a cool brick to the logs that supported the pot, maneuvered the pot onto the brick, then pushed both to a spot where they could eat without getting scorched.

"Very clever," he complimented her, with a crisp nod of his head, then began to eat with a surprising vengeance given his recent snack.

Rory found the food surprisingly tasty, though she attributed this more to hunger than to any deterioration of her taste buds. It was a strangely intimate meal, with few words spoken. They took turns spooning out the contents of the pot between them, quite successfully using the pieces of bark Eric had found earlier. When she'd had her fill, she sat back and watched her companion finish the rest.

"How do you stay so thin, eating that way?" she kidded.

His eyes twinkled good-naturedly. "Oh, I keep busy," he answered vaguely.

"How? You never did tell me what business you were in," she pursued, yielding to her curiosity and taking advantage of his amiable mood.

"Real estate, here and there. Investments. I dabble . . ."

"Where do you work?"

"San Francisco, L.A., New York . . . wherever business takes me."

"Are you married?" The question had popped out quite unexpectedly, and only afterward did she question her impulsiveness.

He raised a hand to stroke his beard. "What is this, an inquisition?"

Rory ignored his question, her green eyes flashing a challenge. "Well, are you?"

"What?" he teased, purposely drawing out her agony.

"Married." She sighed in mock frustration, hopefully disguising her too intense curiosity.

"No." Pure and simple.

"Why not?"

He burst into a spontaneous guffaw, then regarded her with a hint of amusement in his amber eyes that softened his words. "Aren't you getting a little too personal?"

Undaunted, she looked about her at the nest they had put together. "This is a pretty personal situation, isn't it?"

He sat for a moment, staring at her thoughtfully. "You're right," he finally conceded, and mentally she scored one for herself—before she heard his next words. "Who is Daniel?" His voice had lowered several notches, and she knew that she had asked for this. She couldn't very well expect to prod him with questions, without being put on the hot seat herself.

"Daniel?" she repeated quietly, not quite ready to confess that he was her brother.

His eyes pierced her, demanding an answer. "Yes, Daniel."

"I adore Daniel." Her statement was made in a near whisper, though she spoke the truth. She had torn her gaze from Eric and now looked toward the fire, praying that he would not question her further.

"Where did you get this?" he demanded, a harder edge to his tone than before.

Her eyes flew to a piece of paper he had pulled from his jeans pocket and was holding out to her. Hesitantly, she reached for it, opening it up to see the directions she had been following since early that morning. Puzzled at his interest in information that couldn't concern him, she regarded him in confusion. "It's Daniel's. He's working here." She pointed to the general area of the site. "What's so critical about this?" she asked, bewildered at the intensity of his gaze.

"Is this where you're headed?" he asked sternly.

"Yes."

"Why?"

"I'm taking some . . . damn it, that's none of your business," she shot back, unsure at all if she should be telling him anything.

His anger seemed to grow. "But it *is* my business. I'm headed there myself."

"You!" she exclaimed, her fair brows rising in surprise. "Why? You said you were on vacation!"

"I am. Although you may not know it, little one," he began, watching her bristle at the diminutive, "vacations can be learning experiences." It was a typical Charles-type statement, one with which she would have disagreed a year ago, but which she now understood. She held her tongue as he went on. "I, for one, want to see how these glaciologists work. What's your excuse?"

Well, at least he knew what was happening at the X on the map, and that, she decided, earned him some degree of legitimacy. Now it was her turn to justify her trip. "As I started to say before," she told him softly, "I'm taking some supplies to the site." Then her eyes flashed. "The very same supplies, I might add, which you are ravenously devouring!"

He ignored her barb. "Where is Daniel now?"

"Back in Whitehorse." She tensed up. Was he going to start harping on her relationship with Daniel?

"What were you implying about highjacking the jeep?" he accused. "You *didn't* know what was in it, did you?"

"I . . . was only joking." She excused herself lamely.

His eyes narrowed as he studied her. "Rory, I'd like you to tell me what's going on. Now."

Intending only to avoid his harsh gaze, Rory again lowered her eyes to his chest, so broad and strong, tanned and manly. Once again, she was driven by the urge to touch him; once again, she resisted, pivoting abruptly around until she had her back to him.

He, however, was not about to let her escape his sight. With a bold hand on either shoulder, he roughly turned her back, holding her there before him, his victim. "Rory," he growled, "what are you doing?" Silence. "Rory . . ."

Slowly and with much trepidation, she raised her eyes to his. Then, taking a deep breath, she repeated what she had already told him. "I'm taking the supplies to the site."

"I know that," he barked impatiently, his fingers tearing into the soft flesh of her shoulders, painful even through the thickness of her sweater. "What is Daniel's role in all this?"

"He is a journalist, doing an article on the glaciological expedition." She thought she saw a flicker of recognition in his eyes before he dealt her another blow.

"Why didn't he return to the site with you?"

"He . . . had some delay in Whitehorse."

"I don't believe you." His eyes flashed a warning that he was quickly losing his patience.

Slightly impatient herself, she asked, "And just what *do* you believe?"

He looked her right in the eye when he replied. "I believe you may have taken off, without your Daniel's knowledge or consent."

Rory found herself thoroughly intimidated, both because Eric seemed to have intuited the situation so accurately and because he seemed to be so angry. She knew what to expect when Daniel lost his temper; there was the inevitable yelling and pacing, but he had never lifted a finger to harm her. But about Eric's temper, she knew nothing. Wisely, she decided not to test it.

"That's not exactly so," she fudged. "Daniel had to wait around Whitehorse to pick up some fellow, the big shot who sponsored the expedition in the first place."

Something in her words, perhaps her tone of disdain, amused him, though the faint curve at the corners of his lips lingered but a moment as he sobered and eyed her sharply. "And why aren't you back there waiting with him?"

"These supplies needed to be delivered."

He raised one eyebrow. "Rory . . ."

Reluctantly she admitted to a further complication. "He didn't want me to wait with him." She hadn't yet lied outright, though she wondered how long she could avoid it.

"Yet you said he had discouraged you from driving out here alone." He had caught her in a web of her own making, and she had no idea of how to extricate herself. "Well . . ."

"Oh, what difference does it make?" she cried, frustrated at finding herself in this untenable position. With all the force she could muster, she tore away, putting several yards between the two of them. "What difference does it make?" she repeated, growing sullen and once again confused. She could not, for the life of her, understand why he had to know all of this, why he was so persistently pushing her to tell him.

His deep voice boomed back across the short distance. "It makes a hell of a lot of difference. I'd like to know exactly what I've got on my hands."

Now she was incensed, the old Rory lashing back impulsively. "What *you've* got on *your* hands? And just who do you think you are? It's more a question of what *I've* got on *my* hands, since it's *my* jeep, *my* food, *my* will that allows you to accompany me . . ." In her anger, she had risen to her knees, in the posture of a she-cat ready to pounce.

To her utter astonishment, Eric's expression softened suddenly, and a smile overspread his lips. "Come here," he ordered, cocking his head, his tone firm but no longer angry.

"W-what?" she stammered, totally perplexed by the turnabout.

His amber eyes held hers as he repeated his command, this time more softly and definitely seductively. "Come here."

"No." Her voice sounded weak and lacking in conviction. She was aware that she trusted neither his intentions . . . nor her own. The silence between them was broken only by the steady patter of the rain on the roof.

"Rory, come here." He hadn't moved a muscle, yet she felt drawn to him magnetically, his voice, his eyes, his entire being beckoning. Words eluded her; she merely shook her head in lingering denial of his command, a denial which some inner sense knew to be futile. "Rory . . ." He sat on his haunches by the side of the fire, the power of his pull becoming greater and greater. The last shreds of sanity, weak and distant, told her to flee this frighteningly irresistible force. Yet these shreds soon succumbed to the same force, as she slowly stood up and walked to him. It was like being in a trance, aware of what was happening, yet helpless to change its course.

He put his hands about her waist, drawing her closer and pulling her down, until she was on her knees, her thighs and hips in searing contact with his. Before her eyes was the magnificence she had painfully ached to hold. At that instant, she could restrain herself no longer and her hands climbed, shyly at first, to his chest, tracing, then caressing the manly lines and sinews. Her eyes followed the movement of her fingers, marveling at the warmth and firmness of his body, the roughness of his dark-haired chest stimulating her palms.

Her lips quivered with emotion as she lifted her eyes to his once more, her hands now moving up and over his shoulders. There was nothing in his face to discourage her as she raised her lips to his, closing her eyes and tasting the heady wine of his essence, her arms locking around his neck and her body melting into his.

She was unaware of the precise moment when he began to respond, so hypnotized was she with her own uninhibited wanderings. But as his lips parted to receive hers she felt his hands, no longer at her waist, moving suddenly beneath her sweater to the smoothness of her skin, soft and supple beneath his questing touch. She sensed his own ardor as his caresses grew bolder, his kisses more demanding, and it excited her all the more.

His lips left hers to nibble at her earlobe, then moved downward as her head tilted back to allow easy access to her neck. Tenderly, his hand moved to cup a softly rounded breast, and a gasp of unexpected pleasure escaped her moist lips as his thumb traced the circle of its erotic bud. It was as though she would burst from within, so great was the power of this sensation.

As his lips passed her ear once more, she heard his words. "Equal rights, so they say . . ." and before she could comprehend his meaning, his hands had deftly removed the heavy sweater. "Oh, Rory," he murmured, his voice hoarse and low. She sought his lips again, framing his face with her hands, small and slight against his beard. Had she been of sound mind at that moment, she would have judged herself to be a wanton, well versed in the ways of men and their pleasure. Eric had no possible way of knowing that he alone had unleashed, for the very first time, the most primitive needs and yearnings that guided her body.

She felt a pressure easing away as he moved back just enough to reach between them and release the front hook of her bra. It joined the sweater on the ground in an instant, the last remaining barrier. She reached up to draw him once again to her, but he held her back. "Let me look at you," he whispered, the shades of longing in his eyes too strong to defy, the strength of his gaze alone bringing her rosy peaks to their height, her breasts straining upward, her need for him overwhelming.

"Come here," he crooned, his voice passionate and desiring. This time, no repetition was necessary as Rory flew into his embrace, the divine feel of his chest against her naked breasts raising her to another new and hitherto unexplored height. He groaned aloud as their bodies came together, his own arousal as clear in the sound as in the pressure of his manly boldness against her. Her body quaked at the touch, a pulsating current vibrating through her every vein and nerve end.

In answer to her growing need, his hand moved down to her waist, to the line of her jeans, pausing but for a moment. "Eric . . . please . . . please help me," she heard herself beg, the frustration of unfulfilled desire becoming unbearable under his passionate assault. For the first time in her life, she was ready to give, she wanted, no *ached* to give that which was hers alone. Indeed, she would have yielded at that moment, totally and unconditionally, had Eric not instantly and devastatingly withdrawn himself, hands and body, taking her own hands from his neck and placing them deliberately by her sides. His eyes never strayed from her face, pale and stricken, as he spoke quietly and calmly.

"Who did you say was in command here, Rory?" Without waiting for an answer to the rhetorical question, he stood up and moved toward the fire, adding several new pieces of wood before reseating himself on the far side from where she knelt, still in shock.

The flame blazed higher and hotter, yet Rory felt a chill at the loss of his bodily warmth, which had kindled a new and awesome kind of heat within her. She began to tremble, though it had nothing to do with the temperature, as she blindly clutched for her clothing, swallowing hard to stifle the sobs that threatened to complete her humiliation.

four

SLOWLY AND PAINFULLY, THE FACTS BECAME crystal clear in Rory's mind. She had been put down, rejected, humbled in a most cruel and hateful way by a man who, for some reason, despised her. Never once, in her wildest imagination, had she expected anything as traumatic as what had just taken place. She had wanted him so badly her body still quaked. But he had determined to deny her, despite his own arousal, of which she had been so vividly aware during those last impassioned moments. Furthermore, he had been determined to teach her who called the shots in the final analysis. Indeed, he had succeeded. She had helplessly fallen under his spell, and had loved every minute . . . until he had chosen to shatter it so harshly.

Eric saw the look of raw pain, sensed the hurt she suffered, yet refused to give her the satisfaction she had begged for. She struggled to understand the type of man he was, so warm and tender and giving at one moment, so hard and unyielding the next. He had given her a taste of the sweet honey of passion, then wrenched away the nectar from beneath her nose.

She did not understand what made this man, whom she had known for little more than a day, so special to her. All she knew was that he had evoked in her the delight of giving above receiving. Yes, she would gladly do anything, anything for him, so totally had she been captivated. She had never before known the utter happiness so briefly sampled in his powerful embrace. And just as she could not have imagined that ecstasy, so she could not fathom the soul-wrenching despair, the utter desolation which followed.

Staring off into the fire, she wondered if her mother had felt like this when her father deserted them. She had been too young to know the details, too frightened to ask as she had grown older. Was it better to have never known the profound joy of mutual giving than to discover it only to lose it again?

As the evening wore on, she remained locked in this personal battle, wondering this, asking that, debating the other. There were no answers this night, if indeed any existed at all. Once Eric got up to add some logs to the fire, but they remained the most noncommunicatively intimate of strangers. Perhaps he waged similar skirmishes of his own, though she had neither the will to know nor the strength to ask. She knew not the hour when he finally stood, stretched, removed his sleeping bag from the line, and laid it out before the fire.

Had his movement not brought her back to the present, she might have never heard his words.

"We'd better share this. It's going to get even colder before the night is out." Glancing up at him in horror, she found him staring back, hands on hips, as though awaiting her compliance.

But she could not fathom his suggestion, at least not in her present frame of mind. She shook her head slowly. "You go ahead. I'm not tired." She heard the sound of defeat in her voice, yet she was too overwhelmed to care whether he heard it too. Mercifully, he gave her no fight, merely unzipped the sleeping bag and crawled in, back to the fire, without another word. Within moments, Rory heard the rhythm of his breathing steady as, she assumed, sleep overtook him.

Only then did she turn her eyes to his large form, and the ache within her deepened. Impulsively, she stood up and moved to a darkened corner of the cabin, away from the comfort of the flames, yet also away from her tormentor. Here, she curled into a ball and lay brooding and distraught, her eyes all too often flickering in the direction of the mass before the fire. Strangely, she felt neither anger nor bitterness, only the nagging pain of loss.

She lay thus for what seemed hours, her bodily warmth gradually deserting her along with all sense of perspective. In a final attempt at easing her discomfort, she turned her back on its ultimate source, turning toward the cold wall of the cabin. Chilled thoroughly, within and without, she could hold it in no longer. Slowly, the tears formed, gathered, then streamed down her cheeks in silent sobs, wracking her body uncontrollably. She let them come, a welcome release from the emotion that was choking her. She wept freely but silently, her knees tucked up in the fetal position, her arms encircling them, lying on

her side on the cold, cold dirt. She had never cried
for maternal comfort, sought the mother who had
had her own grief aplenty, the mother now dead for
so long—yet she did so now. Only to be held and cradled and comforted . . .

"Shhh . . . shhh . . . it's all right." The arms were
around her, drawing her up into a protective haven,
offering warmth and patience and respite from the
chill. They rocked her gently as she cried, yet now
with a buffer to cushion the pain. A large hand
pressed her head against his beating heart, holding it
there as the tears matted its furry covering. She was
aware only of the release and the comfort, of the
arms that had lifted her from cold despair.

Soft words crooned in her ear. "You're freezing, little one. Let me warm you up." Instinctively, her arms
went around his neck as he lifted her off the ground
and carried her, like a lost child, toward the fire. She
buried her face in his neck, her sobs subsiding under
the steady reassurance of his pulse. She clung to him
as he lowered her, kneeling down himself as he
spoke tenderly. "I want to build up the fire. You're
much too cold, Rory. Stay here. I'll be right back."
She let him disengage her arms, then watched him
get more wood and add it to the fire until a warm
flame danced up once again. When he returned, her
tears had dried, but she was still trembling, from icy
toes to numbed fingertips.

He hugged her cold body to his warm chest as he
commanded softly at her ear. "Don't fight me now,
Rory. You'll be sick if I don't warm you up." Then he
reached for the sleeping bag and moved it close to the
fire. Cautiously, lest she bolt, he removed her heavy
sweater, knowing that his own body warmth could
reach her more quickly without it. Then he tenderly

lifted her and placed her in the sleeping bag, carefully closing it around her.

She had not the strength to fight, nor did it occur to her to as he eased himself down beside her, drawing her snugly against his body, her back to his chest, her bottom to his hips, her knees cradled by his. His hands rubbed her extremities, obstinately coaxing the warmth to flow into them, as his body heat warmed the sleeping bag. Slowly she felt sensation returning inch by inch.

"Better?" he crooned, finally detecting her own warmth; yet he was to wait a long time for his answer as his small and cuddling bundle yielded to the demands of exhaustion.

For Eric, it was a vacation-time slumber, unbothered by the ring of a telephone or the buzz of an alarm clock and lasting for unknown hours. For Rory, alas, it was no different from the many days she'd had no particular reason to arise early. Except that it *was* different. Slowly, very slowly, she opened heavy-lidded eyes to the realization of her position. She lay on her side facing a deadened fire, the unmistakable frame of a man behind her, intimately behind her, one muscular arm under her head as a pillow, the other gripped around her waist. Her legs were intertwined with his, her bare feet warm against his. She felt phenomenally rested.

"So you've finally returned to the world of the living?" The sound at her ear startled her.

"What time it is?" she asked groggily.

"Almost ten." Was that humor, returned again to his tone?

"Ten!" Instantly wide-awake, she flipped herself over so that she could see Eric's face. "Why didn't

you wake me sooner? We should have gone back to
the jeep before now."

He studied her coloring, pleased at the return of a
healthy pink to her cheeks, so ashen the night before.
"You really needed the sleep. So did I, as a matter of
fact. That was a pretty bad night!" It came as a belated
shock for Rory to realize how comfortably she had
finally spent the night and how relaxed and natural
she now felt, half-undressed, sharing a sleeping bag
with this most compelling man whose knee rested so
intimately and possessively between her thighs. There
was something very right about the entire arrange-
ment, yet that fact puzzled her all the more.

"You *do* remember last night?" he asked, catching
her look of perplexity and unaware of its true cause.

She glanced at him briefly, then looked away.
"Yes. I . . . I . . . was upset. . . ."

"You nearly froze to death from your own stub-
bornness!" he barked, though his anger was not as
harsh as it had been at other times.

Quite naturally, though in a totally uncharacteris-
tic way, the words spilled forth. "Thank you." She
held his gaze, the warmth in her green eyes reinforc-
ing her words. It was all so right. . . .

His amber eyes twinkled back at her. "You may be
whistling a very different tune if we don't get up
soon. Listen!"

She turned, puzzled. "I don't hear anything."

"That's it. The rain has stopped. And we'd better
be going." He studied her for a reaction, before purposely creating one by adding bitingly, "We wouldn't
want to worry Daniel. . . ."

Her body tensed at the mention of her brother's
name. He certainly would be worried . . . not to mention furious, should he see her now. Though he had

never lectured her about morals, he made it clear that he had little patience for promiscuity on her part, even less for unwanted complications. "No, we wouldn't," she murmured, absently parrying his barb. To remedy the situation, she made a move to extricate herself from the sleeping bag, only to find herself a firm prisoner of his limbs. Questioningly, she looked toward him.

There was a mischievous gleam in his eye, a devilish twist to his lips as he spoke. "You are fun to sleep with . . . very cuddly. I'd like to do it again. To hell with Daniel."

"You are crude," she snapped back. Then, as she found herself suddenly freed she scrambled out of the sleeping bag and into her blouse and sweater. Perhaps he was being crude, she thought, but she couldn't entirely disagree with his sentiment. She, too, had enjoyed waking up beside him, their bodies touching so warmly and intimately. And through the night, as dazed and distraught as she had been, there had been the constant subconscious awareness of his reassuring presence.

Opening the door of the cabin, she saw that the sun was shining brightly, that it was indeed warmer outside than in. She heard Eric dressing behind her and avoided further temptation by dallying on the front step before returning to help dismantle their cozy nest, repacking the supplies, then heading for the jeep.

Rory did not look back as they left. Only too well did she remember the emotional battle she had waged there; only too well did she remember the pain and desolation that had been felt there; only too well did she remember the intimacy shared there. It was the latter which she chose to cherish, regardless of what the future held, as she kept her eyes forward and followed the footsteps of her companion.

Fortunately, the rain must have stopped soon after they had fallen asleep, and much of the mud had firmed up. The jeep was intact, locked just as Eric had left it the afternoon before. Changing the tire proved to be difficult. However, within a half hour they managed to maneuver back onto the road and were on their way. It had been a kind of unspoken agreement that since they were destined for the same spot, they would continue together. Eric was not at all eager to retrieve his motorcycle, and Rory would have been reluctant to backtrack and lose more precious time.

Within an hour, they reached a roadhouse where they were able to buy hot coffee and pastries, the former, in particular, a delightful treat for Rory, considering her abstinence of the past day. The conversation was pleasant, as each avoided controversial issues out of respect for the subtle truce that had been declared. Compared to yesterday, this was child's play, though Rory was totally satisfied to let Eric do the driving. He seemed fully relaxed and able to handle the gravel road, and she had the freedom to fidget at will, all by way of coping with the steady pounding to her backside. If the jostling bothered Eric, he never complained.

As they rode on, there were interesting sights to break the monotony—had there been any. The landscape was ever-changing: mountains, broad plateaus, forests of spruce, aspen, birch, and the Douglas fir, patriarch of them all. The flatlands boasted explosions of gaily colored wildflowers; the hillsides harbored small bands of Dall sheep, their white coats flecking the green of the slopes. An occasional cow moose could be seen by the swampy mouth of an adjacent creek.

They passed groupings of "spirit houses," structures erected by the local Indians, Eric explained, to shelter their dead in the other life. At Rory's request—motivated in part by the need to stand up and walk around—they stopped by one such cluster, peering through glass windows, cloudy but transparent, to see furs and beads and other trinkets and relics of the departed one's existence.

A bit farther on, they stopped again, this time to explore a small ghost town not far from the riverbank. Reclaimed in large part by the wilderness, the crumbling cabins obscured roads, and rusted implements of the backwoods trapper and the would-be prospector were all there to examine, sparking the imagination with images of a hard and lonely life. Rory found it all fascinating, including the inevitable mounds of tin cans, which spoke of the daily fare of the wilderness man: deviled ham, beans, beef, beans, soup, preserved fruit, and more beans. Signs of deserted campsites dotted the riverbank, dark blackened splotches where fires had blazed, then died or been diligently smothered as the party moved on.

By midafternoon, they reached the site. Rory was suddenly filled with feelings of apprehension, even disappointment, as the cluster of tents came into view at the base of the glacier-scarred mountain. Although she would never have admitted it to him, she enjoyed Eric's company today, found herself more relaxed, congenial, and even likable, than on many another day. It was a new experience for her to be pleased with her own behavior. Although there had been two or three snotty, callous comments that usually characterized her conversation, he did seem to have a knack of bringing out the "best" in her. . . . She did not know how long Eric would be staying at the site, nor how long Daniel would allow her to do so. But there would be chaperones aplenty here, precluding a repetition of the alternately exhilarating and devastating events of the past twenty-four hours.

Eric directed the jeep to the largest of the tents, in front of which stood a table covered with papers, a radio transmitter, and two men. The latter had both come to attention as soon as they heard the vehicle. Rory froze as she immediately recognized one of them. How had he gotten here before her? Had his passenger arrived so soon? He must have passed by the very place where the jeep had been disabled. What was she in store for now?

Daniel immediately recognized the jeep and reached it before it had come to a complete stop, going directly to the passenger side to greet his sister. "Rory! Where in the hell have you been? We've been worried out of our minds! The Mounties are all out looking for you, you and Eric Clar—" He didn't finish his sentence, as a realization slowly dawned amid the worry etched on his brow. But his companion was one step ahead of him as Rory and Eric climbed out of the jeep.

"Eric!" he exclaimed, extending a warm hand to match the broad smile of relief that lit his tanned features. So Eric had been expected too, Rory mused. Blond, bespectacled, and hardy, Daniel's companion shook Eric's hand enthusiastically. "We were worried about you, my fellow. Dan here was waiting for you in Whitehorse when he got your message. A motorcycle?"

Very slowly, the picture came together before Rory's befuddled vision. A picture that explained the lack of concern at consuming supplies earmarked for the site, the anger at discovering the map, the insistence on finding out why she was headed here, and the amusement at her snide reference to the "big shot" behind the expedition. Eric Clarkson . . . chairman of the foundation . . . sponsor of the project . . . now visitor at the site. Her gaze flew to Eric's to see him regarding her closely, smug amusement in his amber orbs. Then she turned to Daniel, strangely reassured to see a bewilderment similar to her own, as he remembered the distinctive face of the man he had caught in an impassioned embrace with his sister in a hotel hallway.

Recovering his composure, however, he extended a hand. "I'm Dan Turner. We're relieved to see you made it." Hesitantly he looked at Rory, then back at Eric. "What did happen to the cycle?"

Briefly, Eric filled the two in on the outlines of his adventure, embellishing on certain aspects of the trip while mercifully ignoring all mention of others. Rory, for one, had not yet recovered from the surprise of his identity and merely stood by mutely as her partner in deception provided a fully adequate accounting of the past day. So that explained the intelligence, the savoir faire, the smooth hands . . .

"So, Dan, your girl here managed to deliver both our supplies and our distinguished visitor," the blond-haired one concluded, as he extended a hand toward Rory. "I don't believe we've been formally introduced, though Dan here has been ranting about you since his arrival. Christopher Winn's the name. Rory, is it?"

"Aurora Matthews . . ." Dan finished the introduction, "Christopher is the leader of the trip," he explained in an even tone, though his hazel eyes were anything but even-tempered as they pierced through her in promise of things to come.

Rory cordially acknowledged the introduction. "It's my pleasure, Christopher," she replied graciously, before turning a puzzled expression to her brother. "But how did you get here so quickly, Daniel?"

He made the effort necessary to disguise his feelings about her presence as he explained. "When we could find no sign of you, I rented a plane and hired a pilot and flew up this morning. There was no sense in remaining in Whitehorse, since I'd received Eric's message and his duffel"—he cast him a dubious look—"and the Mounties were scouring the road from that end. I felt I could be of more use manning the radio from this end."

Christopher joined in again. "Speaking of which, perhaps I'd better advise the troops that you've made it, safe and sound! They may be wondering if the old Walker of the Snows isn't at it again." He grinned before adding, "But he isn't usually out at this time of year."

"The Walker of the Snows?" Rory asked hesitantly.

"He's the genuine ghost of these parts," Christopher explained, his dead-serious expression belied only by the twinkle in his eye. "Very dangerous . . . never a sound . . . never a footprint . . ." Then he burst into smile, a warm and genuine one, and Rory immediately took to the man, who reminded her more of a statesman than a woodsman. She sent him a grateful smile as he returned to the radio transmitter.

"I understand you'll be writing the story on this trip?" Eric's deep voice drew her gaze back to him. As much as she tried to picture him as the prestigious and capable chairman of a multimillion dollar foundation, she could only visualize the enigmatic man who had the power to infuriate and captivate at his fingertips.

Daniel answered him enthusiastically. "That's right! It's a fantastic opportunity to watch these experiments firsthand, let alone have the honor of writing about them. My photographer, Tony Tassinari, is up with the men now. He'll be pleased to know of the arrival of more film." He looked at Rory as he said the last, a slight cutting edge to his words.

Now it was Eric's turn to cut. "It appears that Rory is a valuable young lady to have around!" His amber eyes impaled her before he turned, smiling, to Daniel.

"That she is," the latter agreed politely, "although she'll be returning to Whitehorse tomorrow."

Rory opened her mouth to protest when Christopher bounded back to the group, a broad grin cutting through his blond mustache. "You really had the Mounties running in circles, though they did say something about a ditched motorcycle." He looked at Eric. "They'll have it returned to Whitehorse for you . . . one less worry!"

Without hesitation, Daniel continued. "I was just explaining to Eric that Rory would be returning to Whitehorse tomorrow. As much of a help as she was, bringing the supplies on for me"—he eyed her warily—"she'll only be in the way here."

"No, no, my boy," Christopher argued. "Now that she's finally arrived, I for one see no cause to send her packing. She's a lovely addition to this motley crew!"

Once again, she was startled by the voice at her left. "I agree completely, Christopher!" Eric was speaking. "Why don't we put her to work, Dan," he suggested, a satanic gleam in his eye and the slightest grin on his lips, which warned Rory that he could well complicate already difficult matters for her. "There must be any number of chores around camp that would be best left to a woman. Then you fellows will be freed to concentrate more completely on your work. And what she does will more than adequately pay for the meager amount of food she may consume." His eyes raked her slim form, bringing a blush to her cheeks that she desperately sought to quell. She was aware, however, that the conversation had begun to revolve around her even as it excluded her, and she was not about to let that happen.

"I'd be more than happy to help out, Christopher, if you're sure I wouldn't be in the way. I imagine you all are pretty preoccupied with your work. If I can be of assistance . . ." She could play their game, she told herself, as she flashed an intentionally humble smile in Christopher's direction.

Daniel was now beginning to chafe at the bit. "Rory, I don't think it would be a very wise idea. You have no proper gear, no sleeping bag, no work shoes." He glanced with dismay at her boots, stained and mud-caked despite her efforts to salvage them that morning. "No particularly warm clothes," he went on, adding with a meaningfully forced smile, "and, as I recall"—he looked at the two other men conspiratorially—"you aren't the best of cooks!"

Rory was not about to be put down without a fight, though everything he'd said was true. "As *I* recall, Daniel," she countered, raising her eyebrows teasingly, "neither are you! If, as I suspect, you fellows are taking turns with the cooking, I wouldn't be much worse than some! It so happens that I prepared dinner last night . . . and we neither starved nor died of food poisoning." She turned to Eric, challenging him to disavow her claim. She wondered exactly what he was capable of, given the circumstances. . . .

"I'm sure she'll do just fine," put in Christopher, with an easy and reassuring smile. "She can return with Eric at the end of the week." Then he added to Daniel, "That makes more sense than having the plane make a special trip in!" He turned back to the others. "So it's settled. Rory, you can share Daniel's tent. We've got extra blankets, but I'm sure, with the excess nervous energy he's built up over the past hours, that he can help keep you warm. Tony can move into one of the other tents. Now, Eric, come on over here so that I can show you what we've done so far. We'll unpack the jeep when the others return . . . unless Rory is up to doing it!" He cast her a challenging smile, then placing a strong arm congenially on Eric's shoulder, the two retreated to the piles of papers on the makeshift desk by the large tent.

For Rory it was the moment of reckoning, as Daniel put a firm arm around *her* shoulder and escorted her in the opposite direction, toward a group of boulders that fringed the camp. When he was sure they were out of earshot, he turned to face her. She steeled herself for his attack . . . an attack which never came.

Instead, she found herself looking into deeply emotional eyes, eyes which conveyed fear and concern and relief, with barely a trace of anger. "I was so worried, you little fool!" he exclaimed, as he enveloped her in a hug that nearly knocked the breath from her. He was, indeed, her big brother, protective and caring. She returned his hug as she happened to glance toward the tent to find Eric observing the two of them. Purposely she prolonged the embrace; let him think what he wants, the arrogant beast! "Are you all right?" She nodded. "You sure?" Why did he seem to be looking for something deeper?

"Of course, I'm sure, Daniel. What could have happened? You see me here in once piece, don't you?" she argued quietly, as she sat down on one of the low boulders.

Daniel put his hands on his hips and adopted his wide stance. "What I see above the surface looks fine . . . a little dirty, a little disheveled, but fine. It's what's beneath the surface that worries me." He raised an eyebrow suggestively, but Rory refused to make his task any easier. She merely sat, stubbornly mute, staring back at him. "Did anything happen, Rory?" he asked tentatively.

"Now, what could happen? We took shelter in a deserted cabin and spent the night trying to keep dry, warm, and nourished. What could be more healthy?" Still, she maintained her steady gaze.

"Rory," he began, a touch of exasperation in his tone, "he didn't . . . try anything, did he?"

Her eyes sparked suddenly. "What? The magnanimous Eric Clarkson? Dignified, well stationed, respected . . . molest a poor innocent maiden? No, Daniel, your sister is still a virgin, if that's what you're asking." She gave her brother a look of rebuke at the preposterous idea, though it could as easily have been taken as sour grapes, had Daniel only known the truth. "He didn't . . . try anything," she conceded, more ruefully than she might have liked.

"Well, that's a relief, at least." He sighed, and he did look terribly relieved, to Rory's sudden puzzlement.

She regarded him closely. "You were really worried, weren't you?" she asked.

"Of course I was worried," he barked. "That rain, no sign of you, nothing—"

"I mean, about Eric touching me. . . . I know what your feelings are, but I thought you trusted me in matters like that." She was faintly hurt by his lack of confidence in her.

"I do trust *you*, numbskull. It's him I don't trust!" He cast a scowl over his shoulder in the direction of Eric, who was now busily poring over charts with Christopher.

Rory was now doubly puzzled. Did Daniel know something she did not? "Why do you say that, Daniel?"

Her brother eyed her sharply, his wavy hair so gentle compared to his expression. "I'm not blind, Rory. I saw how he kissed you the other day in the hallway. And, I've since found out quite a bit about him . . . and his reputation."

Rory's breath caught in apprehension. "What about him?" she asked calmly, trying to hide how much his answer mattered to her.

"He's thought to be quite a rogue, Rory. A ladies' man from the word 'go.' And not above breaking hearts along the way." He eyed her inquisitively, and she swallowed hard. But he had more to say before she could respond. "It seems the man is a model of integrity when it comes to business. He's a genius intellectually . . . but a disaster personally. He's already had one tragic marriage—"

Rory could restrain herself no longer. "How do you know all this?" she asked accusingly.

"Christopher told me . . . this morning. It was very tedious, the waiting. He is, it seems, an old friend of Clarkson's, even knew his first wife."

"But why did Christopher want to share all of his dirty gossip with you? Isn't that a kind of betrayal, if they're such close friends?" Her eyes flashed angrily, and suddenly she didn't care if she betrayed her own feelings.

Daniel's tone was calmer. "Take it easy, sweetie.

Christopher was very, very worried. The motorcycle bit was only the latest of a series of potentially self-destructive adventures. According to Christopher, Clarkson has also tried skydiving, hang gliding, race-car driving . . . the more dangerous the better."

"I can't believe it," she murmured, more to herself than to her brother. "He seems so solid and dependable and . . . levelheaded." When she turned, her brother was studying her intently. "What do you know about his marriage?" He had told her that he was not married, but then he'd been playing the same word game as she. She had asked if he were married, in the present tense; he had quite truthfully answered in the negative.

"He supposedly married quite young . . . a childhood sweetheart, who just couldn't keep up with his success. They were divorced after a few years; she committed suicide a year later. At least, that is what Christopher said, and I have no reason to doubt him."

Rory's gaze had shifted past her brother toward the tall, lean figure, now with its back to her. There was so much to ingest, so much to ponder.

"Rory?"

He seemed so strong, so invincible, so calm and practical, able to look a difficult situation in the eye and cope with it. He seemed so immune to human weakness. . . .

"Rory! Where are you?" Her brother's voice was soft but urgent. Only then did she realize that his hands were on her shoulders, as her gaze shot back to him in surprise. "He *did* try his number on you, didn't he?" he accused, suddenly angry.

"No, Daniel!" she denied forcefully. "Well, not exactly . . ." How could she explain what had happened? Here was her brother, whom she adored and who adored her. But something new and different had happened. "I . . . I like him, that's all. He was none of the things you describe. I can't believe we're talking about the same person!"

Daniel stood in silence, regarding her for long moments before gently touching her cheek.

"You seem different, somehow. What did happen in that cabin?"

She shrugged, not sure if she understood it herself. "It was really very much as he described," she bluffed.

"But you do seem different. Subdued. Thoughtful. Not the fiery little prima donna you've always been." Brows knit together, he continued his visual probe, forcing her to look away in embarrassment.

Finally she attempted to put into words, for him as well as for herself, what had happened. "It was strange, Daniel. He was so strong, so protective . . . yet he insisted I stand on my own two feet." Suddenly she smiled. "You can bet I had quite a time cooking dinner, having only recently learned to handle a *traditional* kitchen!" Daniel laughed softly along with her, both of them welcoming the respite from the intensity of their discussion. "He made me . . . look after myself, yet he was right there beside me all the time. He seemed to have a confidence in me . . . though how or why, since he barely knows me and must think I'm a spoiled brat, from some of the things I said"—she glanced at her brother shame-faced—"I'll never know."

Daniel's expression had become almost pained. "Rory," he began earnestly. "Promise me one thing?" She raised her brows, intent on hearing his request before she agreed to anything. "Don't get involved with him. Take whatever happened last night as a passing experience. Don't look any deeper into something that doesn't mean anything. He could hurt you, if he already hasn't, and I don't want that! He's an experienced man where women are concerned, and a potentially dangerous one. Stay away from him, Rory, for your own sake? Promise me?"

"I can't," she whispered. Despite the devastating humiliation she had suffered at Eric's hands that last night, she knew she could not run away. "I'm not looking for anything, Dan, and I hear everything you've said, but I can't promise anything. It's so hard to explain . . . this pull." Then she hesitated. "He insists that I grow up, whereas you refuse to allow it." She bit her lip at the hateful sound of her words, then rushed on to temper them. "Daniel, I *am* growing up. I *need* to grow up. You can't stop it. And I have to be allowed to make my own mistakes, even if I do get hurt here and there. Do you see?" Her green eyes pleaded for his understanding as her hands took his in supplication.

He looked at her adoringly before he sighed and then smiled warily. "You know, for a numbskull, you seem to have developed a sudden way with words." He hugged her robustly, then they headed to the jeep to begin the unpacking.

five

FEW WORDS WERE EXCHANGED AS DANIEL AND Rory carefully removed the supplies. Each was engrossed in his or her own thoughts, miles away yet intimately close to one another. Rory noticed that he did let her do her share of the lifting and carting and stacking and felt she had scored some minor victory. It was only when Daniel broached the topic, as they unloaded the last of the equipment, that she deemed her declaration of victory premature.

"Rory, I've been thinking," he began, seating himself on the open tailgate and motioning for her to join him. "Everyone here assumes that we're lovers. When I arrived here, I told Christopher only that 'my girl' had shown up and that you'd offered to help me out"—this he emphasized with a wry twist of his lips—by bringing the supplies ahead, while I waited for Clarkson."

Rory watched him warily. "And he didn't question the wisdom of letting 'your girl' drive through these roads alone?" It was a reversal of the conversation they'd had that night in Whitehorse.

A private laugh met her question. "He assumes we

journalists to be a little foolhardy to begin with, following a story wherever it chooses to take us. I think he figures you to be a typical hanger-on in the world of the fourth estate." The innocent once-over he gave her was a brief, though subtle reminder of his initial reaction to her presence in this, his personal domain; mercifully, he said nothing to belabor his point. Suddenly, his smile broadened. "Come to think of it, you look about as ill suited for this line of work as Tony, so you just may pass. And, no one will ever suspect the truth, what with the difference in names and all." He paused before making his suggestion. "Why don't we let them believe what they want? At least, it will give you a little added protection. . . ." His voice trailed off as he awaited an impulsive response. But his suggestion was met, not by the childishly indignant refusal he had expected, but by silence, as Rory seriously contemplated the idea.

She had to agree with him. Indeed, hadn't she already subscribed to the deception, knowing full well that Eric had made a judgment that first day back at the hotel? And it *had* served her well, keeping him at more of a distance than he might otherwise have been. She had needed all the help she could get, particularly considering her own total lack of will power when it came to the man's magnetism. She had not lied to him at any point, just chosen her words very carefully. And she saw no reason to change things . . . yet. When, and if, the time ever came, she could then reveal the whole truth.

She burst into a mischievous smile, hugging her brother affectionately. "So we're partners in crime, eh? I think it sounds fine, lover!" And she pressed a quick kiss on his forehead as she stood up. "Now, where do the rest of these things go?"

                              *   *   *

The men descended from the mountain late in the afternoon. There were four of them she had not met, and Christopher rapidly made the introductions with an enthusiasm Rory could not have faulted, until she realized that it was as much for Eric's benefit as her own. She avoided Eric's gaze as, one on each arm, Christopher brought them forward.

"Gentlemen," he began, waving a hand for the men to deposit their gear. "Let me introduce you to our guests." He paused until the newcomers were disencumbered, then proceeded. "First priorities first." He ventured a wink toward Eric. "This is Rory Matthews, Dan's friend, here to help us out for several days. Rory, I'd like you to meet the rest of my crew. Peter LeDuc," he gestured to the redheaded fellow, nearest them. "Peter is out of Juneau. He worked in the Alps last summer; now we are fortunate enough to have him with us."

"Peter," she acknowledged him with a handshake, infinitely grateful for the first time in her life for the experience she'd had maintaining her poise when all eyes were on her, as they seemed to be at that moment.

"Welcome, Rory." He offered his greeting with a friendly smile.

Christopher drew her on to the next man, a pale and rather skinny sort, who seemed totally unlike the others. "This is Tony Tassinari, our photographer. We stole him from his darkroom at the University at Montreal. I sometimes suspect he'd be happier photographing one ice cube than a huge sheet of ice!" He said the last with narrowed eyes, but the friendly hand on Tony's shoulder and the broad grin that followed revealed his fondness.

"How do you do, Tony," she shook his hand eagerly. "Daniel has told me about you. I'm pleased to finally meet you."

"Ditto," Tony smiled, the faintest bit of color rising to his cheeks. Daniel had mentioned that Tony was not the athletic type, but that he had welcomed this opportunity to do something totally different from his usual studio work. Odd, she mused, that he should choose this as a "getaway"!

Now, Christopher led her toward two men of similarly awesome height and build and a remarkable facial resemblance, though one was blond and the other dark. Christopher grinned, seeing the look in her eyes. "Our twins, Brian and Sean McGarraham. They are the true explorers among us, having crossed both poles and lived for a spell in Antarctica."

"Twins?" she exclaimed. "One light and one dark?" Disbelief was written all over her face as she looked from one to the other.

"I'm Sean." The blond ventured forward with an easy grin. "Don't ever confuse me with Brian," he warned, casting a fond glance over his shoulder at his brother. "He's the surly one."

"Only when my brother is remiss in his responsibility," the other retaliated, nevertheless offering his hand. "We are fraternal twins," he explained almost dogmatically, "which makes us no more alike than any two siblings. I only thank God I wasn't made more like my twin; we'd be useless to the world." Rory got the feeling that he almost meant what he said, and she wondered what the story was between the two.

Her arm was suddenly dropped as Christopher moved back toward Eric, who had fallen back during

the introductions. One by one, Christopher introduced him around. Then the group broke up to
occupy themselves before dinner.

"Come on, Rory," Christopher began. "You and I
will be the chefs tonight." Taking her hand in his
large one, he led her off toward the pile of tin cans,
the portable freezing unit, the pots and pans and rustic flatware, and eventually, to the fire.

Christopher Winn was her guardian angel. Under his
tutelage, she learned how to use the camping equipment to prepare a reasonably tasty and doubtlessly
nourishing meal, making her mistakes for his eyes
alone and eternally grateful for that. She was pleased
to find herself a quick learner and more than once
she thought of Monica, dear Monica, whose similar
patience had given her the fundamentals. As she had
in Monica's kitchen, she followed Christopher's
every move with a hawk's eye, praying that when she
was called upon to cope with these primitive conditions on her own, she would be able to rise to the
occasion.

So intense was her concentration that she was
oblivious to the other goings-on about camp. Only
once did she raise her eyes to find a pair of amber
ones disconcertingly following her activity from
across the campsite. Defiantly she held the gaze,
though she wondered whether she did so out of
choice or need. Christopher pointedly cleared his
throat to remind her of her present task, and coloring profusely, she returned to it immediately. She
didn't know whether Christopher had sensed anything unusual in the visual interchange, though she
prayed that he had not.

Daniel, who had disappeared to organize some notes in his tent while she was busy, resumed his place close by her side during supper. Most of the conversation revolved around the many experiments the team was undertaking. She had to notice that Eric was an active participant in this discussion, seemingly understanding all of the technical points that baffled Rory. Since she had no wish to make a fool of herself, she stayed in the background, a position which had definite advantages. It enabled her to avoid the all too distinct possibility of blowing both her cover and her cool. In addition, it freed her to observe the group, the interactions of which she found to be more interesting than the scientific data under discussion.

The team consisted, by rights, of Christopher, Peter, Sean, and Brian, with Tony and Daniel serving as observers and chroniclers of the goings-on. Christopher, at fifty, with numerous degrees and years of teaching under his belt, was the senior member, having spent months planning and researching the tests. Rory marveled at the way he handled the others, subtly guiding as he had with her, yet leaving his companions with a definite sense of individual contribution and power. He was, indeed, the master statesman.

If there was one, Peter LeDuc was Christopher's right-hand man and second in command. Slightly younger, he exuded a kind of dedication, red hair, freckled sunburn, and all, that Rory admired. He listened to Christopher, ingested the other comments, then offered his own, always pithy and to the point.

The twins—twins? Rory exclaimed to herself once again—were a totally different matter. How they ever managed to accomplish all that they supposedly had, she wasn't sure. They seemed to be forever jousting, with the blond Sean on the lighthearted side and the dark Brian his exasperated taskmaster. Watching the two spar she guessed that they must provide a good deal of amusement for the others.

She looked at her brother suddenly, wondering what it would have been like had he been closer to her age. As she gazed fondly at his sandy hair, a mere bit darker and less curly than her own, she was overcome by a surge of affection and she reached over to squeeze his thigh.

Then she quickly straightened, stunned by some unseen probe. Instinctively, she turned in Eric's direction, catching her breath in surprise as her gaze collided with his, the latter harsh and pointed. He had been engrossed in the discussion, or so she had thought, until she had felt the familiar pull. What was he thinking? she wondered. He seemed so angry at her. Had it not been for his rejection of her the night before, she might have attributed his look to jealousy. But that was surely out of the question . . . he had no desire for her. . . .

Now Daniel's arm was around her shoulder, in what only Rory knew to be a brotherly show of affection. "Rory, it just occurred to me. Since you seem intent on staying here" he began quietly, "you could really help me out, if you want, by organizing and typing some of my notes. This discussion reminds me how technical everything is. If you really want to make yourself useful . . ."

"Sure, Daniel, I'd be glad to." She agreed readily, tickled that he, of all people, could finally allow for her usefulness. Then she lowered her voice to a most intimate whisper, "But I'm not a very good typist."

Daniel snickered, rolling his eyes upward. "I seem

to recall two summers' worth of courses on just that skill. . . ."

Rory shrugged. "What can you do . . . I'm incorrigible. All-out addicted to the hunt-and-peck method!"

"Well, whatever, you have to do it better than I do. The portable is pretty limiting, anyway. Besides, it will give you something to do during the day when everyone is up the hill."

"You mean, I can't go? Daniel . . ." She began to protest, only to have their private conversation interrupted by Eric's cool voice.

"Excuse me, Rory. If it wouldn't be too much to ask, could you clean up after this mess? I'd like Chris to show me around a little, since we still have several good hours of light left." His eyes, more dark and brooding than she had ever seen them, sent her a simultaneous challenge and warning. Now that he had revealed himself as the money and the power behind this expedition, she could not very well refuse his request, particularly as he had chosen to issue it in front of an audience.

She was more than happy to do her share; that was what she had wanted all along. It was the way he had approached the issue just then that made her bristle. She wasn't quite sure what was behind his anger, but she could be angry—and crafty—in her own way. If she was going to be stuck with the dishes, she would make sure she had a fun time of it. Looking around at the men, she immediately knew her answer.

"You beat me to the punch, Eric," she parried boldly. "I was just about to do precisely that." She stood up to face him pertly, tilting her sandy mass of curls. "There's nothing worse than a messy house, is there?" she added flippantly, her reference to an earlier conversation obvious to none but the two of them. Then she turned, holding her hands together in mock deliberation. "Now, let me see, I'll need a helper . . . Sean, how about it? Can you give me a hand carrying these to the . . . ah . . ." She looked frantically at Christopher for a suggestion. Yes, she could now find her way around a traditional kitchen, efficiently getting cups and plates, pots and pans clean, but the setup here was far from the standard. "The river?" At Christopher's reassuring nod, she felt a glow of victory and began to busily collect and stack the dirty things, then followed Sean toward the river.

Her judgment did not prove faulty; she had picked just the right one to assist her. Sean was an easy-going, happy-go-lucky soul who was totally unaware of the fact that she didn't know what to do. He launched into easy conversation as he automatically began to scrub the plates by the water's edge. Rory played her cards just right, appearing engrossed in his talk as she watched what he did, assuming correctly that all of the men had dutifully taken their turns in this spot; then, she followed his example until all of the things were clean.

Despite the drudgery that kitchen work was always said to be, Rory didn't mind it this evening. She was doing something useful and her companion was thoroughly companionable, entertaining her with anecdotes about this team member or that, all of which she found to be interesting, particularly in light of her earlier thoughts on each of the men.

"That Tony is unbelievable," he reflected, vigorously shaking his head at the thought.

"In what way?" she asked.

They had finished their work and were seated on dry rocks by the water, the clean dishes and pans

piled neatly beside them. It was not even beginning
to get dark yet, so long was the daylight in this northern spot. Sean's blond hair still shone under the sun,
the tan of his skin in sharp contrast. He was well
built and solid, a good-looking young man in perhaps
his late twenties, Rory guessed.

In answer to her question, Sean shook his head. "I
can't understand why he accepted this job. The guy
is afraid of heights!" His brown eyes twinkled humorously, sending them both into spontaneous laughter.

Rory caught herself up quickly. It really was no
laughing matter. "You've got to be kidding!" she
exclaimed. "That's terrible. How does he manage?"

Sean laughed again, though there was nothing
malicious in his response. "He does yoga breathing . . .
deep, deep breaths. It's a miracle he can hold the
camera steady long enough to take any pictures!" He
paused, evidently regretting his last remark. "But I
understand he's an excellent studio photographer.
And good on portraits. Have you ever seen his
work?" Certainly, as Daniel's lover, she would have.
As Daniel's sister, it was another matter.

"Ah, no," she replied carefully. "I don't like to get
too involved in Dan's work. You know, familiarity
breeds contempt . . ." She smiled lamely, and Sean
looked at her in surprise.

"Then what are you doing up here?"

Quickly she sought to cover herself. "I haven't
seen him all summer! That's a far cry from familiarity, Sean." Her reply was apt, yet she struggled to get
back on firmer ground. "And, once in a while, I do
make an exception." Her mind returned to what Sean
had told her about the photographer. "Poor Tony. Is
it really that bad for him?"

Her companion nodded in confirmation. "Your

Daniel has helped him out on many an occasion." Then, seeing Rory's look of puzzlement, he went on. "Daniel's not afraid of anything. He's right in the middle of the climbing every day. He's very good with Tony, talking him out of squeamish situations. He's even taken several pictures, from the most precarious spots, which Tony won't go near."

Worry had now definitely entered the picture and her eyes opened wide. "Sean, is it very dangerous up there?"

He shrugged; how could one judge danger when one courted it so often? "Oh, it's not really dangerous. It's just the unseen crevasses and weakened areas. You can fall, if you're not careful."

Although Sean seemed to have embellished his words with a kind of bravado, Rory shuddered at their meaning. In her selfishness, she had never really pondered the dangers, the specific perils that Daniel courted in his work. But they were real and she might just see them firsthand. A chill of excitement and apprehension passed through her as she considered that possibility.

She returned to the campsite to find Christopher, Eric, and Peter still off on the mountain, Brian and Tony engaged in a game of chess, and Daniel writing furiously in his notebook.

"It comes so quickly," he explained as Rory strode up, "that I have to grab it or it's gone."

"Anything I can do?"

"Just give me a minute. Then I'll show you."

Rory sat down on a nearby rock and took advantage of the lull to study the campsite. The scenery was handsome and rugged, tree beside tree in mottled splendor.

The air was clear and fresh, tinted with the smell of the woods, the fire, and the sweet wild rose. Above it all stood the mountain, craggy, strong, and fierce, scarred by the years yet eternally resilient. Over her head, a flock of Merganser ducks wended their way to some mysterious destination. She caught, in the distance, the howl of a wolf, the tumble of the river's water, the occasional static-filled reminder of the radio, their major communication with the rest of civilization.

"Here, Rory." Daniel interrupted her thought, and she quickly arose to join him, leaning over his shoulder as he explained what he wanted her to do. There were technical notes, social notes, personal notes, and editorial notes to be sorted out. There were fragmentary articles and essays to be typed. She decided to begin right then.

"Are you warm enough?" he asked as she positioned herself on the ground inside the tent, its westerly flap lifted for the last warming rays of the sun. Earlier she had put on her jacket as she had felt the air begin to chill. For the present, though, she was comfortable, and told her brother so.

"How cold will it get up here, Daniel?" she asked timidly.

"Oh, I doubt it will dip below forty degrees tonight. Having second thoughts?"

"No, sir," she whipped back. "Just wondering." And without another word, she began to hammer slowly away at the typewriter, her toes tucked beneath her, her fingers warmed by their activity. Soon it began to darken noticeably, necessitating an end to her typing. Setting the typewriter aside, she arose and rejoined Daniel outside the tent. He too was putting his papers together.

"What happens now, Dan?" she asked, observing

that the others had disappeared into their tents, leaving the fire to burn down to orange-red embers that perfectly duplicated the color of the setting sun.

Daniel pointed to a pile of blankets. "Those are for you. We'll be turning in now. Why don't you go inside . . ." He grinned and whispered, ". . . to await your lover."

Playfully, Rory kicked at his shin. "I can't go to sleep this early! I'm not in the least tired. After all, I didn't get up this morning until ten—"

Immediately she realized her blunder, as did Daniel, whose features hardened noticeably in the instant. His voice was a low growl when he spoke. "Around here, we rise early and retire early. You do what you want. I'm tired and would like to get some sleep. Please don't disturb any of the others. They are as tired as I am." His tone was tautly controlled; she knew he had made a concerted effort to hold back many words he may have wished, in more private circumstances, to express.

Rory decided not to provoke him further. "Ah, maybe I'll just stay out here a little longer," she suggested, even the dying fire holding more attraction than a pile of blankets.

Daniel abruptly took her arm. "Rory, are you waiting for someone?" The implication was obvious, and it infuriated her.

"Of course not, Daniel. What an asinine thing to ask!" Her green eyes lashed out at him along with her words.

"Is it?" His expression was sad.

"Better still," she thought aloud, truly wanting to be by herself for a little while, "I think I'll take a walk down to the river."

To her surprise, Daniel gave her no argument.

"Here, take my jacket. You'll be cold otherwise." He reached into the tent and withdrew his down parka, draping it about her shoulders and thereby making her look even more tiny and vulnerable than she was. "Are you sure you'll be all right? Would you like me to come?" he asked, strangely touched by her smallness.

Rory smiled gratefully at him. "No, thanks, Dan. I'd really like to be alone for a bit. I've had constant company since yesterday . . . could use a break." Then she added, with a confident squeeze to his hand, "I won't be long. Sweet dreams!" She turned and retraced her steps to the riverside.

As she wound her way carefully along the narrow path, she realized that Daniel would be just as perplexed, right about now, at her words as she was. Alone . . . Rory Matthews wanting to be alone? The Rory Matthews in Seattle never wanted to be alone. The more the better in her entourage! Not so, here in the wilderness of the Yukon. She had suddenly felt that she just wanted to be by herself. Not to think, though there was certainly enough to ponder. Not to plot her next move in some invisibly charted game. But just . . . just . . . to *be*.

She felt it as soon as she sat down on her rock by the water. The peace, the serenity, the feeling—for the first time in her memory—of having earned the right to sit and enjoy. Had there been any brooding thoughts in her mind, they were washed out of sight by the swirling waters, glistening silver on navy as the moon played on their surface from between the aspens.

She remembered the waters of the Yukon River at Whitehorse and her instant response to this land. It had been correct, she mused. More had been demanded of her in the last day than had ever been demanded of her before. And she had given, perhaps not perfectly, but she *had* given. It was a feeling of satisfaction that cushioned her now against the cold night air . . . and Daniel's huge jacket. Yes, she had been right to force her way up here, and like it or not, Daniel had at least accepted her decision.

Her gaze traveled along the meandering riverbank. Suddenly something caught her eye and she gasped in horror at the sight of a cluster of ghostly luminous skeletons waving in the breeze. Her heart pounded within her as she sat, frozen, unable to take her eyes from the unearthly gathering, until a small owl, hooting softly from one of the silver limbs, broke the spell, and she immediately recognized the source of her terror as a group of birch trees, their bark reflecting the moonlight in the most haunting way. Clutching a hand to her chest, she slowly calmed herself, a bit embarrassed at her fright.

"Is something wrong?" The voice was low and right by her ear, having come unheralded through the night woods. Rory jumped up and whirled around an involuntary cry escaping her lips—instantly smothered by a hand over her mouth. She had only to scent the nearness of him to recognize the intruder.

The hand came away in time for her to whisper a breathless, "Eric . . ." before her knees buckled. As she rested her forehead against one palm, a strong hand slipped beneath the neck of the loose jacket to massage the tensed muscles of her neck and upper back, while another supported her in an iron grip.

"My God, Rory, why are you so uptight?" If he had intended his surprise appearance as a joke, there was no humor in his voice now, just raw concern, which Rory noted with pleasure.

"You terrified me!" she exclaimed, her voice several notches higher than usual. She looked into his eyes, lit by the moon, as he knelt beside her, then looked away as quickly in exasperation.

"You were frightened even before I spoke."

"What gave you that idea?" She struggled to steady her breathing, no simple matter in this man's presence.

"I've been watching you since you got here. . . ."

"You've been what?" Fright quickly turned to anger as she rasped at him, "What right have you to disturb my privacy?"

"No, no, little one," he reproached her, standing as he did so and thus emphasizing the diminutive. "It was *you* who disturbed *my* privacy, since I had been here long before you arrived."

"B-but . . . I didn't see you!"

"Obviously, not."

"I thought you were still up on the mountain with Christopher and Peter." She really had not wanted to see him, reluctant to have to cope with his particular form of temptation.

He cleared his throat impatiently, looking from side to side. "As you may or may not have noticed, the daylight is gone. We didn't plan on spending the night on the mountain, you know," he mocked her.

"Too bad . . ." she murmured under her breath, rising to move to a safer distance from him.

"What about you, Rory?" The note of mockery was still there, as he readied for the kill. "Why aren't you back at camp, curled up beside Daniel, warming him the way you warmed me not so very long ago?"

It was a lucky thing she had put a space between them or she would have slapped him. She did not understand why he tormented her so. "You're disgusting!" she seethed.

"Not disgusting." His deeply masculine voice was quiet and complacent in a way she found even more maddening. "Just jealous. I keep asking myself why Daniel should have all the fun, and I haven't yet found an answer."

But Rory had fixated on that one word, barely hearing those that followed. "Jealous? What on earth are you talking about? Jealous?" In her ire, she had stalked up to him, hands on her hips. "I seem to recall that you had your chance, bud, and you blew it!" She'd had no intention of saying any such thing; it had just come out.

A smile broke out on his face, straight white teeth reflecting the brilliant moonlight. "I choose what I want, little one," he began, and Rory was suddenly uncomfortable. "Last night, I chose to teach you a lesson, and as *I* seem to recall"—he emphasized the words in echo of her own—"I succeeded." He paused, watching her cringe beneath him. "Tonight is a different matter altogether. . . ."

Weakness returned quickly to her knees, though she willed herself to stand. Her pulse began to race, her insides to tremble, and she was suddenly overcome by fear. He wouldn't . . . or would he? She was vitally aware of him, standing tall and lean before her, the moonlight adding a sheen to his dark hair, a glitter to his beard, and a spark to his eye, that lent a wicked cast to his overall dark form. She didn't want him to come near, to touch her. She couldn't bear to be led on, as she had been on that other occasion, only to be dropped on a whim. Not here . . . not now! Would she be able to resist her own body's betrayal should he come closer?

Growing more and more alarmed at the look on

his face—desire, lust, need, it mattered not which—
she slowly backed away, afraid to turn, afraid to take
her eyes off him for one instant. He had already
shown her that he could take control of her, mind
and body, if he so desired, Please, no, Eric, she
begged silently at first, then gradually aloud.

"N-no . . . stay away . . ." In answer to her plea, he
merely took a step toward her. She continued to back
away, holding out her hands, as though it would help
ward him off. "Please, leave me alone, Eric . . . I beg
you," she whispered frantically looking to either side
for sign of the path. But she had miscalculated drasti-
cally, finding herself flat against a broad tree trunk.
The only thing to do was to make a break and run. . . .

She had barely begun to pivot when she found
herself roughly knocked against the trunk of the tree,
one strong thigh against her own, holding her in intimate imprisonment. "Let me go!" she cried as she
pushed at the massive chest before her. In the next
instant, she found her arms imprisoned by his, held
back against the tree to either side of her.

His voice was low and husky. "Why do you fight
me, Rory, when you know as well as I do how it will
end?"

"No . . . no . . . please don't." Her moist green eyes
pleaded with him in the darkness, but he paid no
heed.

"You want me, Rory," he crooned, releasing one
hand to trace the curve of her jaw. "You could be
back there with him, but instead you came out here
alone." He outlined the soft curves of her lips. "You
want me. Can you deny it?"

"Yes," she whimpered with the small vestige of
sanity which remained. For already his magnetism
had taken its toll, his nearness tugging at her in the

most forbidden direction. "I deny it." Her eyes were glued to his beseechingly.

"Do you deny it?" He leaned closer, speaking against her lips, not touching, but tantalizing with a breath's caress. She struggled to keep her lips from parting in anticipation of his kiss. Her breathing was short and fast, her limbs wobbly. "Do you?" he demanded, softly insistent.

Her will and resistance disintegrating bit by bit, she could only muster a weak nod, barely perceptible amid the quaking of her body. She gasped uncontrollably, then closed her eyes and turned her face away in ecstatic agony as she felt his hand, inside her jacket, running ever so lightly along her thigh, over her hip, beyond her waist and middle, to outline the firm roundness of her breast. The ache within grew and grew, with each feather touch, threatening to explode into passion-sparked eruption. Tears sprang forth, tears of frustration and confusion, tears of battle between the mind and the body. But Eric had been right; she had, deep inside, known all along how the battle would end. Each and every time her own body would betray her, as it was now doing.

"Will you deny it?" he asked once more, his voice a hoarse murmur against her ear. The tears streamed down her cheeks as he took her chin and turned her face to his. He waited, ever-close, ever-intoxicating, his body propping up her weakened one, until her need for him triumphed and she succumbed to his heady masculinity.

"No," she sobbed quietly, shaking her head. "God only knows I want to, but"—the tears fell with a fury—"I can't."

He waited no longer as his lips descended to possess hers, in a kiss born of hunger above all else. She received it and returned it in kind, her own insatiable hunger within his spell. Both of his hands were inside her jacket now, touching and caressing her, creating a sweet torture, indeed, with their sensual massage. She threw her arms around his neck, clinging to him, her lips, her tongue in passionate dialogue with his, aware only of the glory of his body, so firm and manly and undoubtedly aroused, against hers.

"Rory, where are you?" It was Daniel's voice, calling, still at a distance but coming steadily toward them through the woods. Eric's body stiffened against hers, as they both stood still, all movement stopped, save the pounding of their hearts in thunderous syncopation.

"Rory . . . are you here?" He was getting closer.

"Damn!" Eric swore softly, standing back from her, only his hands on her shoulders as they both struggled to calm the ragged breathing that threatened to betray them.

"Rory?" He was almost at the river. Eric released her with a gentle nudge to start her away from him, while he moved in the opposite direction.

"I'm over here, Daniel," she called, moving as far away from Eric as possible, reaching the water's edge just as her brother emerged into the moonlit clearing.

"Rory . . . thank goodness. I was worried! You've been gone so—" Then he saw Eric, leaning casually against a tree, and he stopped in his tracks. "Rory?" he began, not taking his eyes off Eric. "Are you all right?"

"Sure, Daniel! I . . . just had a fright," she explained, thinking quickly as she steadied herself and walked over to put an arm around his waist. "Fortunately, Eric came along to talk some sense into me. . . ."

"That was fortunate," he replied curtly. What was even more fortunate, Rory knew, was that he had not seen her face as she had spoken those last words. Evidently, thinking quickly in situations like this was not her forte. If Daniel only knew the truth . . . if she only knew the truth. . . .

Slowly, Daniel turned his probing gaze to his sister. "What sort of fright?"

"Come on," she suggested lightly. "I'll tell you on the way back to camp." And, as the two of them headed back, Rory told her brother, with the appropriate degree of drama, of the birch trees, their spectral branches, and a lone owl.

six

DANIEL DID NOT FOR A MOMENT BELIEVE HER feeble tale of Eric's arrival at her moment of greatest need, but he did not pursue the matter. Instead, he merely tucked her warmly beneath the heavy blankets, gave her a brotherly kiss good-night, and turned in himself. Rory couldn't help but note the position in which he had placed his sleeping bag—directly across the front entrance of the tent—assuring him advance notice of all comings or goings, a sad statement, in and of itself, of his opinion of her story.

Infinitely grateful that he did not further the humiliation Eric had begun, Rory gave no argument the following morning when the entire team prepared to leave for the glacier without her. In point of fact, she wanted the time to think about what had happened and was continuing to happen to and within her, and Eric's company, even in a group, was not something she felt she could handle just then. It had been bad enough at breakfast, watching him prepare with the others for the day's outing. Mercifully, though, he ignored her.

The morning sun warmed the air, enabling the men to leave their heaviest jackets behind in favor of the wool plaid ones, corduroy shirts, and cotton turtlenecks over long johns. As Daniel dressed, Rory had all but broken out in a sympathetic sweat.

One of the others prepared breakfast by the time she joined them, though she quickly lent a hand—before a certain someone could demean her by demanding as much. The men seemed well trained, each piling his dirty dishes in a large plastic bin. Rory could only stand by and watch, puzzled as to exactly what she would be able to do.

Finally, spotting Christopher off by himself with a pile of papers, she ventured to broach the subject of her dilemma to his understanding ears. "Christopher . . ." she began hesitantly, "have you got a minute?"

Immediately the large blond head turned in her direction. "Anytime, Rory. What can I do for you?"

She grinned impishly. "It's kind of the other way around. What can I do for *you?* I'll be here all day waiting for you fellows to return, and I'd be glad to do anything that needs to be done."

"For starters,"—a deep voice growled at their left—"you could go over and help Brian pack the lunches. Then"—it continued, amber eyes piercing her relentlessly—"you can wash the breakfast dishes. It may take you a bit longer today," he predicted with near pleasure, "since you'll have no—ah—helper to do your carrying. You may have to make several trips. After that, there's the matter of airing the tents and the sleeping bags. Anything else, Chris?" The eyes did not leave hers for a moment, searching for her reaction.

Christopher had a mild reaction of his own. "That's plenty, Eric. Isn't it overdoing it a bit?"

"Not if Rory wants to earn her keep. She certainly won't do it by sunning herself on the hood of the jeep . . . or spending hours typing her . . . Turner's notes," he snapped acidly; then he turned and stormed away, leaving a heavy silence in his wake.

Throughout his tirade, Rory kept her mouth purposely shut, terrified at what she might yell out in anger at him in front of Christopher, who turned to her, shaking his head in bewilderment. "I wonder what *that* was all about," he murmured.

"I can imagine," Rory replied very softly, staring in astonishment.

"Hmmm?" Christopher asked absently, his eyes, too, following his friend.

She whispered a frustrated "Oh, nothing!" before deliberately returning to the topic that had created the whole scene. "Now, then, let me get started," she offered, and began to move off as Christopher gently caught her arm.

"Listen, Rory, you don't have to worry about all that! We're not fanatics about cleanliness around here . . . and, as I recall, neither is Eric." Once again, his gaze turned in the direction Eric took, a puzzled look clouding his features.

Ignoring the last phrase, she insisted firmly. "No, no. I'd be glad to do it. I'll get as much done as I can," she said, then added with a mischievous twinkle in her eye: "You never can tell. I may even have time for a little sunning on the hood of the jeep." And tilting her tawny curls back proudly, she headed for the table and Brian.

*   *   *

Everything he had so imperiously suggested, she did—though she had far from an easy time of it. For one thing, Brian was a much less cooperative teacher than Sean had been, thoroughly intimidating her with a scornful, "Aw, come on, now!" when she packed the soft sandwiches at the bottom of the sack, then nonchalantly dropped oranges in on top.

For another, Eric had been right about the dishes. Working alone, she had to make three trips down to the river and back, carting egg-crusted and fat-coated plates, charred pans, and coffee-stained cups. By the time the utensils were clean, *she* was filthy! That made trip number four to the river, to wash the clothes she had so unintentionally ruined. Perhaps there was some purpose after all, she mused, behind that most staid of all staid inventions—the apron! For tomorrow, she vowed to improvise one.

Airing out the tents and sleeping bags was just fine; and, yes, she did lounge against the jeep for a while—primarily out of spite, though the sunlight felt divine. The trouble came when it was time to remember which sleeping bag came from which tent. No name tags, no particular color distinctions, and therefore no ostensible way of remedying her blunder. Greatly annoyed with herself, she rolled each one up, then threw them into a pile, determined to let the men cope with that particular problem themselves.

By now it was midday, and she was fatigued from her unaccustomed activity, though she readily conceded that a restless night added to her tiredness. Deciding that some nourishment was in order, she rummaged through the storage bins for some suitable luncheon fare. But cooking anything meant cleaning up, and cleaning up meant another trip to the river, and that . . . was not worth the hunger. So, settling for several slices of almost stale bread, an orange, and the last of the breakfast coffee, she headed for Daniel's typewriter and the piles of notes that awaited her attention.

With this activity, she would at least be on somewhat familiar ground. Unfortunately it was also hard ground, and her back had begun to ache before she'd finished a page. Swearing soundly at herself, she hefted up the typewriter and was on her way to the table by the large tent when she tripped over a large tree root and was sent sprawling. Panic-stricken and with tears of frustration in her eyes, she hastened to check the typewriter for damage, relieved to find it dirty but intact. Her knee, however, was not exactly intact; the knee of her denims was ripped and blood was seeping slowly out.

First aid had never been her forte; in fact, she had been known to pass out at the sight of blood . . . particularly her own. She recalled the time when she was eight or nine and had been showing off her sparkling new bicycle to her friends when she accidentally slammed into her mother's new car. She had fainted, though now she wondered whether it had been more from mortification than from the sight of her blood. That time she suffered a gashed lip, bloody nose, and deflated ego. This time, fortunately, she got off more easily, and she calmed herself with this thought as she searched through the supply tent for a first-aid kit.

By the time the first of the troop returned late in the day, she was thoroughly subdued, physically drained, and not in the best of humors. Yes, she told herself, she had wanted to make herself useful, but was it always so difficult? It was as though the dark one with the amber eyes had put a curse on all of her good intentions, forcing her to work doubly hard for each little bit of success. And it was to continue. . . .

"No, no . . . not that way, Rory." Sean's gentle voice chided her as he rounded the bend just ahead of Peter and Brian and rushed over to the fire she was trying to get going. "You haven't got the logs arranged right—they need breathing room," he explained, as he made the correction, then took the matches from her hand. "My God, what did you do to yourself?" he asked, suddenly eyeing the ragged red blotch at her knee. Silently she cursed herself for forgetting to change.

"Oh, it's nothing." She laughed feebly. "I tripped and scraped my knee." Actually, it had been more a gash than a scrape, and it stung like hell, she realized.

"Have to watch your step there," he kidded her. "We don't want to lose a potentially great firemaker!" He laughed as he stood up and squeezed her shoulder, then turned toward his tent.

Stiffly, Rory stood up also. But there was to be no respite just then, for into sight came Tony, Christopher and—to her shock—in mutual conversation—Daniel and Eric. She made no move toward them, afraid of limping visibly, but simply stood and forced a smile.

"You look terrible!" It was Daniel speaking first, as he came close enough to catch the pallor on her face.

"I do believe she's had a hard day." Eric smirked, mockingly eyeing the disaster at her knee.

But it was Christopher who made the reference explicit. "Whatever happened, Rory?"

At last, she sighed, turning and grinning sheepishly. "I tripped. It looks worse than it is!"

The worry was evident on Daniel's face. "Let me take a look at it," he suggested, kneeling down beside her to pull apart the torn knee of her jeans.

Gingerly, she stepped back, becoming more embarrassed by the minute and beginning to wonder whether this minor fiasco was indeed going to turn out to be another bike-against-the-car ordeal. "No, no," she protested quickly. "I've already bandaged it."

"Did you wash it first?" The amber eyes flashed at her dubiously.

Raising her chin a little higher, she assured him. "I certainly did. I wouldn't think of bandaging a dirty wound."

Now it was Daniel, wearing at her dwindling patience. "I can't seem to remember your ever bandaging anything! Now let me see!"

"It's all right, Daniel," she insisted angrily, moving toward Christopher. "I think I did everything you wanted," she told him softly, determined not to give Eric the public satisfaction of knowing that she had actually done what _he_ had wanted. "I only made one gross mistake." She lowered her voice. "I aired all the sleeping bags, then forgot whose was whose."

All eyes turned to the huge pile of bags, beside which Sean was already standing, scratching his head in puzzlement. "That's beautiful," he exclaimed, bursting out into a hearty guffaw. Rory could have sunk into the ground.

"No problem . . . each one has an identifying mark, which you had no way of knowing." It was Peter, dear Peter, coming to her rescue, and she marveled at how all of the others had let her suffer, even for those few long seconds.

As Peter sorted the sleeping bags, Eric stepped forward menacingly, speaking in a voice loud enough for all to hear. "Where's supper?"

She whirled around, wincing involuntarily as her knee rebelled against the sudden movement. "Supper?" He hadn't listed that among her duties; why hadn't she thought of it herself?

"You know"—he tormented her—" the meal that one eats at the end of the long, hard day?"

She began to bristle at his tone, that tone of voice that could put her in her place so effectively. But, if he was chipping away at her pride, she still had plenty of spunk left. "I think I know what it is, Eric," she retorted testily. "But I had no idea what delicious menu you fellows had in mind for this evening. And"—her tone hardened even more—"since I've had a long, hard day myself, a little assistance would be very appropriate."

Suddenly he grinned sadistically. "So it was a long, hard day, was it? Not used to such rigors as dish-washing?" In front of the entire group, he had chosen to humiliate her. But, she vowed, she was not going to let that happen. A hurt inside now joined the one at her knee as she squared her shoulders and took a deep breath, willing away the tears in her eyes.

"No, not under these conditions. And I readily admit it. But I tried. And I think I did a passable job. Now, if you'll excuse me, I'll see to dinner." She turned to the others, her voice growing less angry, though no less forceful. "Sean, will you please keep an eye on that fire you started. Daniel, you can come with me to choose the menu and help cook it. I have several things to say to *you*." Without another look at Eric, she stalked off, oblivious to the pain in her knee and the slight aberration of her gait.

She was also oblivious to the comment that Christopher made to Eric when she had gone. "I do believe you've met your match in that little lady, friend!" Then he too turned on his heel and left Eric to his own dark thoughts.

Poor Daniel, however, was to bear the brunt of Rory's anger and frustration. "Why didn't you say anything? How could you let him humiliate me like that, Daniel!" she fumed at him, as soon as they were inside the supply tent.

"He's not such a bad sort."

Rory blinked in disbelief at her brother's words. Was that Daniel talking? "Come again?" Certainly she had heard wrong.

But Daniel's voice was loud and clear. "I have to agree with what you said yesterday, Rory. I rather like him."

"I can't believe you're saying this . . . after the cabin, last night, this . . ."

He seemed amused by her reaction. "You tell me that nothing happened between the two of you, and I believe you. You're a big girl now, Rory. And I think Eric's got the right attitude. You seem to feel that you're missing out on things . . . like roughing it. It's not as exciting as you thought, is it?"

"Were you two talking about me today?" Her eyes narrowed in angry suspicion.

"We didn't have to. His opinion of you is right out front for all of us to see." He chuckled at his joke, the humor of which Rory failed to see.

"Rrrr . . ." She gritted her teeth in fury. "The whole lot of you are impossible!"

"No, sweetie," her brother contradicted her claim. "It's *you* who are impossible at times. Now, let me see your knee, like a good girl."

Her fury erupted without restraint. As Daniel knelt down once more to examine her leg she kicked with all her strength and knocked him over. "Not on your life!" she snapped, pointing to the open flap of the tent. "Get out," she growled. "I can do very well without you!"

Slowly her brother grinned. "I thought you'd never ask," he drawled, then he ducked out of the tent in time to avoid further blows. She had indeed cooked her own goose, literally and figuratively; on that thought, he laughed aloud and headed for his tent.

Someone at least was on her side. This time, it turned out to be Tony, a most unlikely candidate, whom she had guessed would be as inept at things culinary as she was. Not so, she was soon to discover.

With his help, they managed to present a most passable dinner, again with Rory picking up hints here and there from her "assistant." Christopher appeared at one point to observe the preparations, though she sensed somehow that it was she he had primarily wanted to observe. His smile was reassuring, as was the fatherly hand on her shoulder.

Mercifully—and most probably due to Christopher— she was relieved of cleanup duty. Brian and Peter assumed that chore while Christopher challenged her to a game of checkers.

He was, she noted again, the consummate statesman. No sooner had the two of them entered his tent in search of the checkerboard, than he turned to her and insisted quietly but firmly: "Let me take a quick look at that knee before we begin."

Coming from anyone else, she would have staunchly protested. Coming from him, she welcomed the attention. Her knee was doing any number of uncomfortable things. At his urging, she sat on the ground while he gently raised her pants leg and removed the dressing. She gasped as the gauze tore away from the wound.

"Whew!" he exclaimed, poking lightly around the gash, "that must have been quite a spill. Let me get some disinfectant. I'll be right back." He disappeared, leaving Rory to fight the queasiness that the sight of the oozing mess had reawakened. Taking several deep breaths, she looked away, intent on thinking of anything but the ugly gash. To her shock, her gaze fell on a pair of rich leather boots, then traveled slowly and disbelievingly upward until it rested on a dark and bearded face, with strong lips, a fine nose, and the most compelling amber eyes she'd ever seen.

Eric merely stared at her, from her face to her knee and back again. "You look like you may pass out."

The queasiness had miraculously vanished. "I wouldn't give you the satisfaction," she seethed.

"Are you sure you did that all by yourself," he teased. "It's an awfully big cut for a little girl like you."

"Actually," she snapped, "I was accidentally tackled by a Mountie during a game of touch football."

"What you need, methinks, is a baby-sitter."

"And what *you* need, methinks, is a good night on the town with the local barmaid. Now, get out and leave me alone."

He looked at her long and hard for a moment, his amber eyes icy. "You're right!" he growled. "The barmaid *would* be preferable." And he turned and was gone before she had a chance to get in her own last word.

Fists clenched, she bit at her lower lip to discourage the tears that had sprung to her eyes. Unfortunately, Christopher chose that moment to return, entering the tent sideways, as though he were watching someone outside, then turning to take in her pained expression.

"Sorry I took so long." He glanced once more toward the flap before looking at her face. "Is the pain that bad?"

"From my knee?" She sniffled. "No . . ." Her voice cracked and she felt herself begin to break down. "I'll be all right in just a second," she whispered, inhaling deeply to counter the sobs and covering her eyes with a hand to hide the tears. She was almost grateful for the harsh sting of the disinfectant as it saturated the bruise. By the time Christopher had put on a fresh dressing, she had regained a semblance of composure.

"Are you sure you're up for that game of checkers?" he asked, when she had lowered her jeans' leg and accepted his hand to help her stand.

She nodded, wiping away the last trace of a tear from her cheek. "I think I could use it more than ever. Something to take my mind off . . ." She let her voice trail off, catching herself before she betrayed her inner feelings. She couldn't explain to herself, let alone Christopher, the hurt she had just suffered at Eric's words.

Christopher looked at her thoughtfully before proceeding to set up the game on the table outside the tent. He let several moves pass before he broached the topic. "What's going on between you and Eric?" he asked quietly, his tone carefully calculated to reach no ears but hers.

"Between me and Eric?" she repeated innocently.

He said no more, but regarded her calmly, awaiting her response. "Nothing . . . what makes you ask that?"

Christopher made his move on the checkerboard before he answered. "Your face just now. I thought it was all on *his* side. I've never seen him behave this way to a woman." He talked ever so softly and his eyes were filled with concern. "But he was in here just now . . . and it was written all over your face."

Quickly, she looked away. "He despises me, for some reason," she murmured, feigning concentration on her next move.

"Despises you? I doubt that, Rory." Christopher's voice chided her gently.

"Then why is he always tormenting me?" she whispered, her eyes involuntarily betraying her pain.

"Maybe it's because he is tormented so himself." Christopher held her gaze now, the game temporarily forgotten.

She looked at him in confusion. "What do you mean?"

"Eric was married once—"

"Yes, I know," she interrupted, though he seemed not at all surprised that she should have known this.

"It was a very unhappy experience for him." He hesitated, lost in his own thoughts and recollections.

"But what can that have to do with his behavior toward me?" Her green eyes challenged his with a boldness of old.

"Wait. I'll show you." As Rory looked on in bewilderment he disappeared into the tent, returning moments later with his wallet in his hand. Reseating himself, he flipped through numerous credit cards and identification cards, to find a small, dog-eared snapshot, which he handed to her.

Understanding was instantaneous when Rory saw the two faces on the photograph, and she gasped aloud. "Oh, my God . . ."

"Yes, Rory, you look exactly like her. It's uncanny."

"How do you come to have this, Christopher?" Her voice was a shaky whisper.

"Donna was my niece. She and I were very close."

Rory was silent for a moment, staring down at the wedding picture of a much younger and clean-shaven Eric Clarkson and his radiant bride. "They looked so happy. . . ."

"They were, for a while. Then, very slowly, it fell apart. . . ."

"I'm sorry," she whispered, so strongly identifying with the girl in the photo that she felt a deep sadness course through her veins.

"They both suffered." Christopher, too, shared the sadness as he spoke. "Perhaps Donna was lucky. Her suffering ended. Eric's continues. Oh, he hides it," he added quickly, anticipating Rory's disbelief, "and he buries himself in his work, but he can't seem to find that peace . . ." He had been talking on, almost forgetting Rory's presence for the moment; now he looked up in surprise and cleared his throat in sudden embarrassment at what he had so casually revealed. "I think it's your move," he ventured unsurely. As Rory followed his gaze to the checkerboard he turned the conversation around. "And what about you?"

There was no question about what he referred to, and she made no pretense to the contrary. She shrugged, still keeping her eyes downcast. "I don't know. It's all so confusing. . . ."

Now his voice was nearly inaudible. "What about Daniel? Do you love him?"

Her head shot up in instant response. "Of course I

love him. He's my broth—" Her word was cut short as she realized what she had said to this most paternal and understanding man, and she prayed that her assessment of him would prove correct.

It was Christopher's turn to study the board, stroking his mustache as he digested her words. "Your brother? I should have realized—"

"Please don't be angry with him, Christopher," she whispered beseechingly. "He didn't want me up here . . . I more or less forced myself on him . . . and it just seemed safer to let people believe what they wanted." He made his move, calmly jumping two of her men. Then he rested his elbows on the table, folded his hands, and pondered. For Rory, his pause was pure agony, as she wondered whether she might indeed have just blown Daniel's assignment for him.

"But his name is Turner, yours is Matthews. Why the discrepancy?"

Hoping to regain his trust through honesty, Rory explained. "I took my mother's maiden name, as she did when she and my father were divorced. Daniel kept Dad's."

He nodded thoughtfully, apparently accepting the explanation. "How long were you planning to keep up the deception?" He was neither angry—to Rory's relief—nor amused, but strangely objective about the whole situation, Rory did not know whether to be disturbed or comforted by that fact.

Again she shrugged. "Until I leave, I guess." Then a disconcerting thought hit her. "You won't say anything, Christopher, will you?" Her green eyes were like a child's, wide and pleading.

For the first time in the discussion, he smiled. "No, Rory. I won't spoil your secret. But it definitely is humorous, the more I think about it."

Her brows furrowed. "In what way?"

He looked at her warmly, a mischievous twinkle in his eyes. "I do believe that Eric is as jealous as hell of your Daniel!"

"It's good for him, the arrogant wretch," she replied, now remembering only the notorious ladies' man rather than the star-crossed lover. The gentle humor in her eyes belied the stern tone of her voice.

"You may just be right," her opponent agreed, as he nonchalantly jumped two of her kings to effectively win the game.

Jealousy. Eric himself had mentioned the word to her. Then Christopher. In her wildest imaginings, she could not have believed it to be true. As she had told him once, he had had his chance and had rejected her. Of what could he be jealous? He knew he could manipulate her, and in that sense he had everything he wanted. He could decisively put her down, again and again, and he knew it. That was how he seemed to get his satisfaction—or was it revenge?

Now there was a new element in the picture. Eric looked at Rory and remembered his ex-wife, his beautiful childhood sweetheart, now dead, though very much alive in his thoughts. Did that explain why he seemed to want to punish Rory . . . to make up for all the punishment he had suffered, either through loneliness or guilt, over the years?

Tired as she was, Rory lay beneath the blankets for minutes that stretched slowly and agonizingly into hours. Christopher had asked the question, "And what about you?" She honestly did not know that answer. She liked Eric . . . sometimes. She found him to be fascinating . . . usually. She bristled at his insolence . . . often. She was powerless to resist his magnetism . . . always.

That she craved him physically was no longer a question, but a fact. But was it enough? He was, ironically, so much like Daniel. He seemed to want to subjugate her, and that was what she could not have. Nor, she added in light of her recent discovery, could she have him relating to her as a memory which haunted him mercilessly.

There were the other things—the tenderness and understanding, the intelligence and wit, the determination and confidence, both in himself and, yes, in her. All of these were positive things, all of these seemed to drive her inexorably toward some unknown destiny quite apart from that of a sandy-haired bride so long ago.

Grasping for the truth amid the maelstrom of emotion, Rory realized that she adored the man, that as much as she told herself otherwise, she looked forward to seeing him—even when he humiliated her so cruelly. She adored him, pure and simple, and would continue to do so despite any amount of pain he inflicted in his heartless lack of adoration for her. Therein lay the greatest pain of all.

Whether or not she finally dozed off, she couldn't remember, when a sound close by disturbed her and two hands descended to awaken her.

"Are you asleep?" the voice whispered in her ear. Her head flew up in surprise and fear, and she would have cried out had she not quickly recognized that distinctively musky smell that had been burned into her memory.

"How did you get in here?" she whispered back in

bewilderment, looking at Daniel's sleeping form by the tent flap.

"Shhh! He sleeps very soundly. You must wear him out!" The voice had a touch of sarcasm. "Come on out for a minute. I want you to see something."

"What are you up to?" she asked suspiciously.

"It's just for you. Come on." He took her warm hand in his and gently urged her up. "Only for a minute. Come on . . . I'll be on good behavior!" His whisper was so sincere, humor and all, that she found herself unable to refuse. Trying to make as little noise as possible, she carefully climbed out from beneath her blankets and crept after Eric, her hand still firmly grasped in his, over Daniel's form and into the cool night.

Eric did not need to direct her attention. She gasped as soon as she saw it. It was the sky, flowing and swirling, sweeping and shimmering in a nocturnal arabesque of color: greens melding into violets, pinks becoming oranges, then blending into reds. It was truly an awesome sight to Rory as she stood there, Eric a hair's breadth behind her.

"What is it?" she whispered, awestruck.

"The aurora borealis, the northern lights," he explained softly by her ear. "They are seen more often in the fall, but I suspect they made an early appearance for their namesake!"

"It's fantastic!" she exclaimed breathlessly, unaware that her body had slipped back against his as she tipped her head back to watch. His hands slid lightly around her waist, and although she didn't notice that either, she was aware of a thorough peace within as she was enchanted by the miracle of nature without.

Suddenly a shudder passed through her. "Are you cold?" he asked gently against her hair.

"No. It's just that . . . I feel so insignificant all of a sudden . . . like a tiny nothing in this huge universe. . . ."

"You aren't exactly what I'd call a 'tiny nothing,'" he teased.

Her eyes remained glued to the heavens as she tried to explain further. "I mean . . . we have so little control. Something as magnificent as that up there . . . we can't start it or stop it . . . it's . . . frightening!" She turned within the feather circle of his arms to look up at his face. Had he understood what she was feeling?

"Many things in life are like that, Rory." His deep voice was soft and patient. "There are those things in nature, such as the aurora borealis, over which we have no control." His amber eyes flickered up at the northern sky, then returned to her emotion-filled face. "And there are those things in the human experience over which we are similarly powerless." As she gazed up at him in wonderment he bent his head to place one ever so brief, ever so tender kiss upon her lips. Then he turned her and headed her back to her tent. "For that very reason, little one, I think you should go back to bed now," he whispered. "I just wanted you to see. . . ."

"Thank you." She mouthed the words silently, in a quick turn of her head to see him one last time before the tent flap obliterated his own heavenly form from view.

seven

Rory was to have plenty of time to contemplate his words the next day, for Daniel flatly refused to allow her to accompany the group to the glacier.

"Why not?" she had asked him angrily.

"Because it's dangerous! You were a walking catastrophe down here yesterday. I can just imagine what would have happened up there," he replied, stifling her objections for the time being.

Christopher suggested that she take inventory of the supply tent to determine what food would be needed during the next in-town stop, and she was grateful for the suggestion, even though she suspected that Eric may have been behind it.

As for the latter, he spared her not a glance during breakfast, only approaching her as the first few men started on the trail. She was stacking dishes for her first trip to the river when the low voice rang out behind her.

"Very domestic," he taunted, in reference to the

large towel she had commandeered to serve as an apron.

She stared at him for a long, disappointed moment, having expected a little more thoughtful comment after the moving experience of the past night. Piqued, she snapped, "If all you can do is tease me, you'd be better off making yourself useful. Here"—she thrust a stack of plates at him—"take these down to the river for me, like a good boy." Then, in her most dramatic manner, she threw her curls back as she bent to pick up the rest, then marched ahead of him without so much as a glance to see if he was following.

Sure enough, no sooner had she set her load down by the waterside, than a second pile materialized beside it. She made no comment as she smugly began to scrub, and it was only when she turned to stack the clean plate on a dry rock that she noted the casually lounging form against a tree.

Squinting up at his backlit form, she scoffed, strangely annoyed, "Haven't you got anything better to do? Or are you just dying to dry dishes?" She had to admit that her annoyance was mostly due to her own reflexes, the way her heart began to pound, as it now was doing, whenever the man came near.

As he studied her an unfathomable expression crossed his features. "You really are a novice at this type of thing, aren't you?" he asked. Surprisingly, there was none of the mockery in his voice that there had been moments before.

"You could say I haven't had as much practice as some," she conceded, continuing with her vehement scrubbing as a way of fighting the electrical energy his presence created.

"Does Daniel wait on you?"

"Why should he?"

"*Someone* has to do the cleaning up."

Rory made no reply. Should she tell him that there were servants to do that kind of work at home? Certainly, in his position, he would have a few servants of his own.

"Do you and Daniel live together?" His dark head had straightened to an angle of alertness, which belied the nonchalance in his voice.

"Of course!" she answered automatically.

The low voice echoed hers, quietly and deeply, "Of course . . ."

It was only the ensuing silence that gave her a chance to reflect on that automatic response. She had blurted out the truth, but inevitably Eric would have misinterpreted it. But should she further enlighten him at this point? No! She had promised Daniel she would keep to the deception and perhaps it could still suit her purpose. Eric was difficult enough to control, without offering a free slate!

Puzzled by the long silence, she paused in her work and looked back at him. He was still lounging confidently against the tree, his strong arms crossed arrogantly over his chest. "Are you going to stand there all day?" she prodded impatiently.

"Any objections?"

"Yes, as a matter of fact. I'd prefer to work alone." Not exactly true, but in this case, imperative. She was not sure how long she could trust herself under his gaze.

And that gaze grew sharper and more troublesome by the minute. "It seems to me," he began, one eyebrow raised, "that your preference is secondary here, since it's *my* project which theoretically employs you."

Even as she inwardly fumed at his attitude, Rory realized that the more she argued, the more he would also. Therefore, she kept silent, willing herself to ignore him. On the surface, she was successful; beneath her poise, she was not, her anger reaching a near boiling point when he finally spoke.

"Do you think you can manage without me?" The mockery was clear in his tone, and was the last straw.

She glared at him in fury. "I've done very well for the last twenty-one years!"

Slowly he sauntered toward her. "Have you?" he drawled.

"Yes, I have," she fairly yelled. Then, as his looming form towered above her she spat out, "Why don't you go pick on someone your own size?"

"Like Daniel?" he asked in a deep, somber voice.

Frantically, she stood up. "You just keep your filthy hands off my—" Miraculously, she caught herself before she had blundered irrevocably. "Leave Daniel out of this . . . please?" Her green eyes pleaded as her stomach churned furiously. Why he could provoke her to such violent extremes of emotion she did not understand!

A devilish smile unexpectedly overspread his features. "You're running true to form," he commented, humor bubbling through his words. Rory looked at him questioningly. Then her gaze followed his to the pile of washed dishes beside her—which, at her abrupt rising moments before, had been inadvertently knocked into the dirt.

Bitten as much by his smug amusement as by her own carelessness, she turned to him, screaming. "Go away! Will you leave me alone for a change?"

He made a slow, mocking bow as he backed off. "It

will be my pleasure. I don't think I can bear to witness any further calamities." Then he threw her a final wicked and infuriating grin as he headed into the woods, thereby escaping the soapy sponge that was hurled in his direction.

After rewashing the offending flatware and finishing up the remaining pans and utensils, she made the necessary trips back to the base camp to stack everything neatly before attempting her next chore. She felt undying gratitude to whatever unknown power caused the rest of the day to proceed uneventfully. She completed Christopher's inventory, made some headway on Daniel's notes, and even had a dinner on to cook by the time the men returned, duly impressed by her newfound efficiency.

She had also had time to think, yet her mind continued in its relentless turmoil right into the evening, making her almost indifferent to the success she had earned that day. He was a most perplexing issue, this Eric Clarkson, evoking reactions in her that surprised, puzzled, pleased, and angered. It was as though she had been exposed to a lifetime of emotions in these few short days.

If her preoccupation during dinner was noticed, it went unmentioned, save for the long and intent glances that converged on her from no less than three separate corners. To these, she was also oblivious, excusing herself quietly after dinner and falling asleep in her tent long before the last orange flecks had darkened to a blue-purple on the fir boughs above. Be it by virtue of exhaustion or escapism, she slept soundly untroubled by the voices that softly discussed her from the tent opening.

"Do you think she's feeling all right?" the tall, dark

one asked, barely disguising the concern in his amber eyes. "She was awfully quiet when we returned today."

His companion, with whom he had spent a pleasant evening of stimulating discussion, turned his hazel eyes toward his sleeping sister, his smile warm and affectionate. "She outdid herself today, I think. It's good for her, even though I have to admit I was against her coming in the first place," he whispered.

A different, more disturbed look passed briefly over the bearded face before he forced a smile for his friend. "Well, good-night, Dan." He spoke in a controlled voice, then left the sandy-haired man to his privacy.

"Come on, Rory! You're coming with me today. Let's get a move on!" Daniel urged his sister awake with a firm pat to her backside, nearly ineffectual through the layers of blankets under which she had burrowed, but enough to stir her from her sleep.

"Where are we going?" she mumbled groggily, the effects of three nights of minimal sleep having finally caught up with her. Then awareness abruptly returned. "Can I go up there today, Daniel?" she asked, bolting up into a sitting position.

"Uh-uh." Her brother shook his head. "But I'm taking you out on the town!" His grin was broad enough to almost compensate for the refusal.

"On the town?" she asked incredulously. "What are you talking about?" She smoothed unruly curls off her face as she eyed him askance.

"Actually," he explained, only slightly apologetically, "I have to send a report off, so we're taking the laundry shift while we're at it."

Rory's heart dropped. "The laundry shift?"

"Yes, my dear. How do you think we all manage to look so debonair? There's a woman who does the laundry for us in Ross River, but we have to get it to her by ten, or she won't have it ready for us to bring back. Let's go!"

She was left open-mouthed as her brother headed to get some breakfast. Anticipating a more "civilized" day, and desirous of having her own dirty clothes cleaned also, she dressed in a pair of brown corduroy jeans and shirt, topped by a beige Irish-knit sweater, another of Doris's suggestions that proved to be a godsend. The outfit was smart enough, but her major concern was to locate the nearest hot shower she could find in town, and she loaded her bag up accordingly.

The admiring eyes that turned her way when she approached the others were not lost on her this morning, and she acknowledged them with an easy smile as she took the dish of pancakes and the cup of coffee that was handed to her. Only one face was stern, and that one she avoided as much as possible. She insisted on doing the breakfast dishes herself before they left, thereby ruling out her lack of diligence as the cause of Eric's glare. Indeed, the scowl was deeper than ever as she climbed into the jeep and Daniel headed for the road, leaving her with its memory imprinted on her brain, to be carried with her through the day.

Mrs. O'Hara not only took the laundry in with a smile, but she also firmly insisted that Rory use the bathtub in her own home, an offer Rory was not about to refuse. Thus, while Daniel worked between the post office and a telephone booth, she soaked luxuriously in a hot tub, laden with the bubbles her benefactress had so graciously provided. It was pure heaven to her, having, since she left Seattle, forsworn such delightful pastimes. The fresh smell of her skin, the renewed gleam of her hair, the moist glow on her cheeks—all made her wonder anew whether she could ever be a real outdoor person. Then she thought of Eric as she fluffed her damp curls over her shoulder, sprinkled herself liberally with cologne, and set out in search of her brother—as confused as ever.

True to his word, Daniel escorted her to the fanciest restaurant the small wilderness town had to offer, a none-too-fancy home-style place with a simple menu and more simply delicious food.

"Does it always taste better when someone else cooks it, or is this just so much better than the food we've been eating?" she asked tongue-in-cheek.

Daniel laughed heartily. "Now you're sounding like a seasoned woman of the house." Then his sandy head steadied and he eyed her seriously. "What have you thought of the past few days?"

Rory thought for a moment, her eyes playing on the water glass. "It's . . . been an experience!" she said softly, as serious as her brother and hard put to find one word to sum up her feelings.

"Is that good . . . bad . . . indifferent? You were so eager to come up here," he reminded her.

In Rory's mind, that discussion in Whitehorse could have taken place an eon ago. So many new frontiers had been crossed since then, yet she was hard pressed to say whether any had been conquered. It was so perplexing. . . . "Oh, a little bit of each," she finally admitted.

He studied her features with an interest she couldn't and didn't want to ignore. She welcomed this opportunity to talk her feelings over with someone.

"A little bit of each?" He repeated her words as she slowly tried to gather her thoughts.

She shrugged, with a shy smile. "A little good . . . a little bad . . . a little indifferent." Never had shyness been a factor before her brother; this was a new experience to join the others.

"Okay," Daniel began patiently, as the waitress brought them each a large stein of beer. "Start with the 'indifferent.'"

There was no hesitation as Rory explained this, the most straightforward of her reactions. "Dinner . . . dishes . . . cleaning . . . inventory . . . typing . . ." Then she as readily qualified her judgment. "Actually, I can't say those things leave me totally indifferent. The work itself *needs* to be done but is a rote chore, the same thing over and over again. There is a certain satisfaction to be gotten . . . I suppose . . ." Her voice trailed off as she recalled the pride she had felt at having been able to complete these "rote" chores, not to mention the anticipation of approval from a particular quarter. . . .

When she made no move to elaborate further, Daniel proceeded to the next of the categories. "How about 'bad'?" Again he waited patiently, watching Rory fiddle with the remains of her meal as she chose her words.

"The humiliation of bungling a job, like the sleeping bags, or the squished sandwiches, the embarrassment of those skeletons by the river." She blushed as she smiled in remembrance. "My knee . . ."

"Life is full of experiences like that . . . they're not so 'bad' in the long run," he argued softly.

She looked up, nodding slowly in agreement. "I know, but in front of . . ." Her voice trailed off. Mercifully, her brother chose to let it ride.

"Okay. Let's hear the best, the 'good,'" he urged, surprised to see his sister's face take on a sad, almost pained expression. He frowned accordingly as they sat in silence, and he wondered suddenly whether she now regretted having come in the first place.

"The 'good,'" she repeated thoughtfully, raising a slim finger to absently twist a soft curl, a childhood habit she had decidedly suppressed, but which chose this time to reappear. Daniel, in turn, was touched by the memory of the very sensitive, very vulnerable little girl who had, over the years, constructed a sturdy facade of self-confidence and self-ishness around herself. "I'm not sure how to explain it," she began quietly, her gaze avoiding his self-consciously. "The sense of doing something, or justi-fying my existence, the feeling of an earned exhaustion at the end of the day, the thrill of a chal-lenge faced head-on . . ."

Now he rebuked her gently. "But you've had any number of challenges. . . ."

"I seem to recall your saying, not so very long ago," she retorted with a sly grin, "that those kinds of challenges were quite different." Then she became more serious. "You were right . . . as were Charles and Monica. They are very big on different kinds of challenges. They would be proud of me, if they could see me now." A poignant smile gentled her lips as she thought of her friends.

But Daniel's thoughts were of another person. "And where does Eric Clarkson fit into your three-way scheme?" His voice was much lower, more intense, and she wondered for a moment whether he was angry . . . until the affection in his hazel eyes out-shone the vocal inflection, and she relaxed once more. "Is he good, bad, or indifferent?" He grinned.

Rory threw her head back and laughed, her sandy curls bouncing gaily back into place when she looked again at her brother. "Not indifferent, I can tell you that much!" She giggled, sensing a return of the shyness that had touched her earlier.

"What else can you tell me?" It was the older brother, alias father substitute, who prodded her now.

Painstakingly, she tried to piece together her thoughts, something which she had failed to do for several days. "I like him. I don't like him. He excites me. He infuriates me. He fascinates me. He exasperates me." She hesitated, turning beseeching green eyes to his for help. "What can I say? I don't understand any of it!"

Daniel took her hand in his, much as he used to do when she was smaller, and patted it consolingly. "Growing up is tough!"

"Oh, Daniel!" she shrieked, "Don't make fun of me! I'm not a child. I'm twenty-one, a legal adult."

"Shhh," he quieted her, noting that several hometown heads had looked up at the sound of annoyance coming from this unusual-looking young lady. "I'm perfectly serious, Rory. And I think that you are too . . . about Eric."

A look of shock crossed her face, then sadly she shook her head. "There's so much about him that puzzles me. And I know so little about his life when he's *not* on vacation."

Daniel sent her a look of mock surprise. "Since when were you so concerned about all the details? He's a very respectable person, Rory. We've had some good talks. I've already told you that I like the fellow. I also admire him and trust him."

Rory looked on in genuine surprise, while her brother championed his previous enemy.

"You know that he sponsored this expedition." Rory nodded at the obvious. "Do you know that he has also sponsored other scientific projects?" She shook her head. It had occurred to her that he had only done this on a whim, to ease some of the guilt he felt toward his ex-wife's family, of which Christopher was a prominent member.

Daniel elaborated. "Last year, it was funding a grant to study the effects of offshore oil wells on the potential cultivation of undersea protein gardens; the year before, it was a study of the problem of hazardous waste disposal. He is a committed environmentalist."

Rory was duly impressed despite herself. "Where does he get the money to back these studies?"

Without batting an eyelash, Daniel repeated at length the story that the man himself had much more modestly told him. "He's truly a self-made man, Rory. He started on the ground level when he was seventeen or so, working for a neighbor in his hometown who had a small scientific instrument business. He went to college at night while he learned the business by day. He quickly built it up into a national corporation—greatly expanded in scope, needless to say. By the time the owner died, Eric had stock in the company and money to buy more, thus enabling him to take a controlling interest. That was eight years ago. He's gone international and has expanded even further since then." He paused in appreciation of the man's feat. "Quite a story, isn't it?"

Slowly Rory nodded. "Very different from ours . . ."

Her brother knew immediately what she meant. "It's all been very easy for us."

As the waitress removed the dishes and brought them each a steaming mug of coffee, they remained silent, their minds similarly regarding the lives of ease and comfort that their parents had afforded them.

"So we look for our challenges elsewhere." Rory broke the silence finally, putting into words what her brother had also been thinking. "You have your work, and I have . . ." She yielded to the silence again, finding herself at a loss for words.

"He's quite a challenge, little sister!"

Rory's head shot up in surprise at the subtle twist of the conversation. There was nothing of mockery, nothing of anger, only good-hearted humor and sincerity. But if she was taken off guard by his words, she was bowled over by his next ones.

"I think we should tell him the truth, Rory." The silence was more intense than any of the others had been.

"A-about us?" she croaked in disbelief.

"Now, what other truth would we have to tell him?" he chided her gently.

"No!" Her refusal rang out firm and instantaneous before she even considered her brother's proposal.

"Why not?"

At a loss for an immediate answer, she countered it with a question of her own. "Why should we?"

Daniel contemplated her taut features before he responded, calmly and reasonably. "I think that he has a right to know. He is very involved—"

"The project has nothing to do with this," Rory interrupted hurriedly.

"I'm not talking about the project, you fool."

She ignored his taunt, her eyes narrowing as suspicion dawned. "Have you been talking to him about me again?"

Daniel's denial was immediate. "No! I've never

talked to him about you. That's just it. He avoids the topic like the plague!"

"He hates me!" Hurt was written all over Rory's face, though her eyes remained dry and her lips steady.

"My lord, Rory, you can be dumb!"

"I'm not being dumb," she denied vehemently. "Can't you see the way he orders me around, taunts me, humiliates me, then ignores me whenever he can . . . and in front of all the others!"

"Rory . . . Rory . . . listen to me!" Now the tears had appeared and Daniel took her hands in his and attempted to enlighten her. "Rory," he spoke, his voice full of confidence and conviction, "you are so involved yourself that you can't see what's happened. If Eric hated you, he would never have gone out of his way to do those things. It's totally out of character!" Rory was listening, though distinct skepticism shadowed her features. "Rory, he's jealous and he's angry. He assumes that we're lovers. He's jealous of me and angry with you—that is the root of his problem . . . and yours."

She could almost have believed him, this pillar of stability whom she had adored for years and years. But there was that little bit that he did not know and she did. She shook her head in misery. "It's not that simple, Dan. You see, I had this talk with Christopher the other night . . ." and she proceeded to tell her brother about many years of unhappiness and an uncanny physical resemblance.

Daniel listened thoughtfully, frowning as he sipped his coffee. When she finished, she bowed her head and whispered timidly, "What should I do, Dan?"

"I can't tell you that, sweetie," he answered softly. "I'm no psychoanalyst. I can't judge whether what you've told me is significant or not." Then he looked at her pointedly. "Do you want to pursue it?"

She knew the answer, as she had known it forever. Mutely, she nodded her head, her green eyes round with earnestness, tawny lashes luxuriantly framing them like halos.

"Then I still think we should tell him."

"No!"

"Why not?"

"I can't"

"Why not, Rory?"

"I'm . . . afraid!" That much was obvious from the look of anguish in her eyes.

"Afraid of what?" Afraid of what? Afraid of what? The words reverberated in her brain. "Rory, whatever are you afraid of?"

Anguish became bewilderment as she sought the answer to his question. "I don't know," she murmured. "Him . . . me . . . I don't know!" She raised pleading eyes to his. "I do know that I feel safer this way, with you as a buffer. Just give me a little more time . . . please!"

Whether Daniel fully understood her fears, Rory couldn't tell. The more she thought about it later, the more she saw that she was terrified of losing control . . . as she was all too prone to do in Eric's presence. Until she knew what she really wanted, she had to keep a semblance of distance, regardless of the vital yearnings of her own body. She had to keep a distance. . . .

"Okay, sweetie," her brother agreed gently. "We'll keep it up until you feel ready." Then he hesitated, as though debating an issue within himself. "But, Rory, will you promise me something?" Her eyebrows arched questioningly. "I think that Eric is drawn to you. And I think that he could make you very happy—" He held a hand out to silence the protest, which was forming on her lips. "Hear me out, Rory! I trust Eric. It's an instinctive thing. I want you to always remember that he's there should you need help, even if nothing more ever comes of . . . your relationship. . . ."

"You sound so morbid, Daniel," Rory finally blurted out, swallowing hard to dislodge the lump in her throat.

"We've become friends, Eric and I," he reiterated. "Do you promise?"

Eager to dispel the sudden and unusually oppressive mood, she conceded, "Yes, Daniel, I promise."

eight

THE NEXT MORNING, RORY ACCOMPANIED THE men up into the mountains. She wore her sturdiest clothes, from her sneakers to Daniel's extra wool jacket, with blue jeans, a bulky turtleneck sweater, and a shirt beneath, all chosen for warmth as well as for comfort.

In her naïveté, it had not occurred to her that it would take any effort to reach the glacier itself. What she had not counted on was an hour of brisk hiking over narrow paths twisting up the craggy mountain-side. What she had not counted on was the slick grass at the lower levels, into which the hiking boots of the men clamped firmly but on which her tennis sneakers slid mercilessly. What she had not counted on was the unstable gravel obstacle course to which the grass yielded as the altitude increased and on which she seemed to take one step forward for every two that carried her back. What she had not counted on was the grueling pace of the men, well accustomed to the climb and eager to get on with their research. She quickly found herself at the end of the caravan, then ten yards behind, then out of sight. And according to her rough calculations, they were but halfway there! Exhausted, she collapsed on the nearest rock to catch her breath, a feat complicated by the thinning air.

"Tired already, Aurora?" The deep voice penetrated her weariness as it played deliciously over the syllables of her full name. It may have been the high altitude that made her giddy. It may have been precisely the sound of her given name spoken on this man's tongue. Most likely, it was a combination of the two that set her off into a gale of impish laughter.

"This is absurd!" she exclaimed between peals. "My legs seem to have gone on strike!" She giggled again, making no move to rise, but rather shading her eyes from the morning sun as she looked up at the dark face, which, to her relief, appeared to share her amusement. "How much farther is it anyway?" she asked.

"I'd say," he began, rolling his eyes skyward in mock calculation, "that you have about six more slips, four more slides, and a possible ten all-out collapses until you get there!"

Again she burst into a fit of laughter. "And how did you get stuck with the battle zone?"

He laughed gently at the reference to her own deficiency. "I'm afraid I volunteered." Then he paused, eyeing her as his tone changed. "I'm pleased to see that you have a sense of humor!"

"I don't really have much choice, do I? I can either laugh or cry . . . and I have a feeling that I'm going to look disastrous enough by the end of the day without big puffy red eyes!" Slowly she stood up, moaning dramatically as she did so. "Lead the way!" she exclaimed, as she came alongside and awaited his movement. He nodded his head, cocking his eyebrow in surprise that she was ready to move on. Then he turned and led the way on up after the team.

If Rory thought she'd had trouble before, she would never have let herself in for what was ahead. Now there were boulders to be mounted, narrow chasms to be jumped. Worst of all were the strong, broad back and well-muscled legs just ahead of her, which distracted her dangerously from the most serious business of watching her step. Her palms were scratched and aching by the time Eric took mercy on her and led her over the more tricky spots.

As it turned out, Rory would have endured any amount of hardship for the glory of the patient attention and gentle assistance Eric showered on her. This was indeed the Eric she could adore, and she loved every minute of his company, rewarding him with broad smiles and an eager hand, not to mention a total absence of snappishness. She found herself wishing that the glacier was even farther off, if only to prolong this time with him. His hand was firm and strong in hers as he guided her, his thigh muscles braced against the slippery rock as he eased her up and over a sharp boulder. She clutched desperately at his forearm as she leaped across a narrow break in the rock, then laughed in relief as she found herself safely grounded by his side.

Miraculously, under his guidance, she surprised them both with her agility, taking but a few of the slips, slides, and falls he had predicted. And as though to reward her for her competence, he made her hand a permanent fixture in his own as his gleaming white smile showered her with approval and encouragement.

The height of delight occurred for Rory just before they reached the glacier. Having climbed a particularly steep area, there was a drop of four feet or so to the path. Eric went first, easily jumping the distance, then turned to help Rory, whose timid leap took her exactly where his hand led her—into his waiting arms.

"Atta girl!" he exclaimed, as he enveloped her in a bear hug. Then he looked down at her rosy cheeks and sweat-dotted nose. "You do pretty well for a novice!" He beamed proudly as he lowered his head and placed a gentle kiss on the tip of her nose.

As for Rory, she was enjoying Eric's attention too much to pay any heed to the aches that were the usual plight of the novice. She accepted his kiss excitedly, her green eyes luminous and bright, her arm around his waist, her body drawing renewed strength from his. "I try," she murmured with a shy grin, wishing desperately that he would kiss her again.

"You certainly do," he complimented, a look of admiration in his glowing amber eyes which thrilled her even more than the exhilarating view from the heights around them. As if reading the desire in her eyes, he turned her fully toward him, and cupping a finger to her chin, he raised her lips to meet his for a briefly sweet and enchanting taste, then ever so tenderly released her and, leaving one arm across her shoulder, led her onward.

The moments were precious. Had Rory had her way, she would have bottled and preserved them for time immemorial. There was no fighting, no taunting, no undercutting or jockeying for power. There was a pure companionship, a sense of oneness with each other and with nature. Indeed, she would have bid the "civilized" world a permanent farewell, just to keep this most peaceful feeling.

"There it is," he murmured against her hair, as they mounted the last rise and came within sight of the glacier, stopping still to savor these last ·moments of privacy. Ironically, when she should have been bounding forward to finally see what she had waited for so long to see, Rory could not take her eyes from Eric's, so warm and responsive. He was positively divine when he set his mind to it, she mused, as his arm slowly slid from her shoulder and he reluctantly stepped back.

"The others will be looking for us. We'd better let them know we've made it." He spoke softly and sensibly, not for a minute taking his eyes off Rory's.

She nodded slowly. "Okay," she whispered, only then dragging her gaze away and toward the open expanse of ice, over which the men were scattered in small groups. "It's huge," she exclaimed in awe as they moved forward. The chill from the packed ice beneath their feet could just as easily have been caused by the loss of his touch, but she coralled her attention toward the glacier.

Eric seemed to have felt the chill also, his face grown strangely taut, though his voice retained its warmth. "This is tiny, actually, compared to most." He paused to wave briefly at Christopher, who had looked up from his work to acknowledge their arrival.

Rory focused on the men, one after the other. "What are they doing?" she asked, wrinkling up her nose in puzzlement and thereby drawing a spontaneous smile from her designated teacher.

"There are several different projects within the larger one," he explained patiently. "Basically, glaciologists want to know whether the size of the glacier is changing, and if so, in what direction. The trend so far in this century, in mountainous areas such as this and the Alps, has been for a retreat, a melting down of the ice." He put one arm around her shoulder and turned her slightly as he pointed with the other in the direction of Peter and Sean. "Do you see those stakes? They have been driven into the ice at various points. By measuring the changes in their positions, Chris and his team can then determine the glacier's speed."

Rory was fascinated by this clear explanation of some of the things she had struggled to understand in Daniel's none too orderly or legible notes. "Is the melting very obvious?" she asked.

He shook his head emphatically. "No. As a matter of fact, there are indications that the summers are once again turning slightly cooler, slowing the melting process." He led her forward for a closer look at the work the men were doing, though if she were to be truthful, she would have had to confess her greatest interest lay not in what he was telling her but in the fact that *he had* all of this to tell. Evidently, Eric had not blindly spent the money to fund a project he neither knew nor cared about.

Off to one side, Rory caught sight of Daniel diligently taking notes on whatever it was that Brian was so dramatically describing. Off to the other side, Tony was busily photographing the activity that occupied Christopher. She stayed where she was while Eric became involved in the data Peter was collecting, but he soon returned to her side with a devastating smile of renewed hello.

"Come on." He cocked his head as he took her elbow and guided her to a section of rock where they could sit and watch the proceedings. "I'm glad you have that jacket. It's a damn sight warmer than your short one and better fitting than that parka you wore."

If he was goading her, she ignored the bait, hugging the jacket to her body as she adopted a model's pose. "I'm glad you like it. It's the latest in fashion, straight from Paris—"

"Sit down and shut up." He laughed, grabbing her arm playfully and pulling her down next to him.

They sat quietly for a while, watching the proceedings, before Rory ventured to ask what she feared was a thoroughly dumb question. "What is the overall purpose of studying glaciers? I mean, once you know whether or how much they are melting, what do you do with that information?"

To her instant relief, Eric did not seem at all disturbed by the simpleness of her inquiry. "There are two basic reasons," he explained carefully. "First, any sudden movement of the glaciers could have dramatic effects on our environment. For example, a sudden and complete melting of the Antarctic ice sheet would raise the worldwide sea level by two hundred and thirty feet. You can imagine what would happen to our coastal cities!"

"Is that about to happen?" She gulped at the prospect of her own Seattle being swallowed up by the sea.

Understandingly, he smiled. "No, no! And that would be the extreme anyway. But even a yard of melting can affect sea level. At least if we know what's happening, we can be prepared."

"I see your point," she agreed softly. "What's the second reason?"

"Studies of the overall amounts of glacial ice are important, and may become even more so, because of the dire shortage of fresh water in various areas of the world. There may be the possibility, at some point in the future, of towing large chunks of ice from the poles to those areas that need fresh water."

"It's an interesting concept."

"A very promising one," he added, "for countries plagued by drought!"

Rory's eye was caught by Tony's camera, recording their conversation from a distance. "I think we're being photographed," she informed him in her most mysterious whisper. "Smile!" Impishly, she elbowed him in the side as she pointed in the photographer's direction.

"Hey, that hurt!" he yelled back, grinning as he launched an attack of tickling, which sent Rory, rolling with laughter, into a doubled-up ball. Giggling breathlessly and at the mercy of long fingers that seemed to be everywhere, she was pleading for a truce when he finally relented, hugging her fiercely before releasing her.

While she caught her breath, they sat side by side on the boulder. Steadying her breathing from a fit of laughter was one thing; steadying her pulse from Eric's touch was completely different.

"He's not the jealous type, is he?" he asked suddenly, surprising her with his words.

"Who? Daniel?" She stared at him wide-eyed. His eyes conveyed a confirmation as they bored into her, searching for some unfathomable response. "No, Dan's not the jealous type."

"Does that bother you?" Again, the searching look.

"No." She met his gaze confidently. Then something in his expression reminded her of the power he wielded over the expedition, and her confidence was suddenly dented as her eyes opened wider. "Am I supposed to be doing something? I mean, working or helping?"

He grinned mischievously, and her heart skipped a beat. "You are." Her brows furrowed in confusion as he proceeded to enlighten her. "It's your job today to keep me company. As you can see"—he made a sweeping gesture—"a spectator here can get very lonely."

Rory could think of no witty retort. Her heart thudded and her senses reeled from Eric's charm. She had vowed to keep a distance, yet it was the last thing she wanted now. Surely, she rationalized, she was safe, with all of the team in attendance. Yes, she decided, she was safe, and damn it, she was going to enjoy herself!

"Then I guess I'm at your disposal," she offered, yielding to the here and now. As fate would have it, the here and now was to produce a day of joy, laughter, excitement, passion, and ultimately, despair.

Throughout the rest of the morning, Eric kept her company more than the other way around, providing miscellaneous facts relating to the experiments, describing the other projects he'd sponsored, even sharing his hopes for future expeditions. As much as she questioned his frame of mind where women were concerned, his talk ruled out any doubts she may have had as to his dedication, intelligence, and integrity in professional matters.

Directly after lunch, he exchanged several private words with Christopher and then with Daniel, then he strode toward her and took her hand firmly in his. "We've been excused for the afternoon," he said, a wide grin on his face.

"Excused?" She regarded him skeptically.

"Let's go!" He began to lead her toward the path, but she held back timidly.

"Wait!" She looked hesitantly at Daniel, who promptly waved and sent her a broad smile of permission.

"See." Eric nodded. "I've already gotten his okay. Now, let's go!" He drew her on, over the boulders and out of sight.

"Where are we going?" she cried, as she scrambled to keep up with him.

He looked back, the flame of excitement flickering in his amber eyes. "I've got a treat for you!"

"Please, Eric, slow down! I'll never make it at this rate!"

Mercifully, he did slow down, taking pity on legs that were more used to the smooth and even surface of a dance floor than the rugged terrain of a mountainside. And the return trip was just as romantic, in its own way, as the trip out had been. Once more he was protective and gentle in guiding her, and friendly in a way that sent her to the farthest reaches of hope.

She let herself pretend that there had never been a Donna to whom he had been so unhappily bound. She let herself pretend that there had never been a deception that paired her brother and her as lovers. She let herself pretend that there had never been an impulsive and selfish princess, born and raised to wealth, spoiled, pampered, yet virtually helpless in the real world. Above all, she let herself pretend, for that short time, that Eric adored her as she adored him, freely and unconditionally and from the very soul.

It was merely a matter of time. Rory knew it, as did Eric, from the moment they set off on their own, alone and together on the mountain. The forces drawing them toward one another were too powerful to be overridden, even had one of them tried.

It happened not far from the glacier, about a third of the way back to the base camp. As they rounded a curve in the path Eric looked around mischievously as though searching for a particular spot. Satisfied, at last that he had found it, he drew Rory through a narrow crevass between two jagged rocks, onto a narrow ledge, which was for all practical purposes a dead end.

"Is this the treat?" she asked meekly, terrified by the sheer drop that faced her on all sides.

"No." He grinned. "This is just a sideshow. Isn't it beautiful . . . the view?"

Rory's every muscle tensed. "It's frightening here. That drop is straight down and this ledge is none too spacious!" With all her strength she held back, but Eric's grip was stronger, pulling her out in front of him.

"You do trust me, don't you, Rory?" he asked, as he drew her trembling body back against his and looked out over the countryside from over Rory's head.

She nodded. Yes, she told herself, she did trust him.

"Then know that I would do nothing to endanger you. This ledge is perfectly safe. I just wanted you to see the view." His arms had settled intimately on her shoulders and across her chest. Now she clung to them as though her life depended on it, which, in her suddenly terrified state, she firmly believed.

So great was her fear that she missed the impact of the northern Canadian panorama that stretched all about them. There were the carpeted flatlands and the rolling foothills, the distant mountains bathed in a midday mist of gray and green, and the river, an endless blue ribbon winding in and about as far as the eye could see.

Unfortunately, Rory's eyes did not see very far, as she twisted her head and swallowed hard. "Please, Eric, I'm frightened!" He took one look at her eyes, then promptly led her back to the regular path, where she sank down upon the nearest rock to regain her composure.

"I'm sorry, honey," he apologized, kneeling down beside her, and the ache within her now had nothing to do with the fright and everything to do with the endearment he'd used and the tenderness and sincerity of his voice.

She looked up and their eyes met on an equal plane. He raised a warm hand to stroke her cheek; instinctively, she lifted her own to cover his, then turned her face to kiss his palm. Her action took her by surprise. It had been so natural and heartfelt, yet she cast him a look of apology for her forwardness. She hadn't said a word, yet Eric read her perfectly.

"It's all right, Rory," he murmured softly. "Never apologize for that which is so right." That which is so right . . . hadn't she sensed the same thing before?

When his lips met hers, there was none of the demand for capitulation that there had been at other times. It was a mutual desire, a mutual need that brought them together in a soft and slow embrace. His firm lips caressed her tenderly, exploring and tasting and feeling for the sheer joy of the touch. She responded in kind, as though savoring a new and delightful experience, which was an end in itself, not a prelude to anything else.

It was a lingering, passionate kiss, yet unhurried and relaxed. If possible, it was an even more heady experience for Rory than his more imperious and commanding kisses had been, for this was truly a shared moment, one in which the whole far surpassed either of its parts.

When they drew apart, finally and breathlessly, their hands remained in contact, fingers intertwined as if in poignant tribute to the moment of eternity they had just created and shared with one another.

"Let's go!" Eric whispered huskily. "The best is yet to come!" As they stood up, his arm fell across her shoulder, drawing Rory's side against his own, and they proceeded thus, separating only when necessitated by the terrain. Rory marveled at how easily and snugly their bodies fit together, much as their fingers had meshed and their lips had melted together moments before.

"You've changed," he told her softly as they walked along, the hand on her shoulder giving a squeeze of approval to erase any doubt as to his meaning.

"So have you." She looked through her long lashes at him, studying his ruggedly handsome features, drinking in his masculinity, forming permanent pictures in her brain for her to cherish. He *had* changed, at least in his attitude toward her on this day. It was as though he had come to accept her as an equal. It was as though he had indeed found some inner peace after a long, hard battle.

Yes, she too had changed, she realized, as they proceeded in silence. She had found a beauty in life that had nothing to do with outward appearances. This beauty was intangible, invisible, elusive. Yet she had seen it, touched it, and preserved it—if only in memory. It was the beauty of giving and sharing and . . . loving. She had discovered the beauty of love, that love between a man and a woman which is chosen, rather than inherited, and treasured, rather than taken for granted. She knew that if she never saw Eric Clarkson again, she would love him for the rest of her life, carrying the memory of these precious moments of harmony and happiness with her forever.

Suddenly, it seemed imperative that he know the truth. She could deceive him no longer. "Eric, let's talk," she said quietly, as they rounded a bend to a smoother section of pathway.

"Shhh . . ."

"But I want to—"

"Don't spoil it, Rory," he told her gently. He had felt it too, the very special something that had passed between them. And, knowing only too well that reality would soon be upon them, he refused to waste the precious moments.

"It's about Daniel. . . ."

Eric stopped short and turned around to face her, putting both hands on her shoulders as he looked down imperiously. "No. I don't want to hear anything about Daniel," he barked gruffly, then his amber eyes melted and his voice softened to the deep and husky tone she adored. "We've got the whole afternoon, honey. Let's enjoy it!" There was a certain pleading in his own eyes, and that killer of an endearment, which would get her every time.

She nodded as she gazed up at him, not for the moment hiding the raw adoration in her green eyes. Then, in a last gesture of acquiescence, she put her arm out to circle his waist, and they continued, side by side.

By the time they reached the base camp, Rory's curiosity had grown to overwhelming proportions. "What *is* this treat?" she finally burst out, unable to keep her peace any longer.

He grinned, that sparklingly devastating and slightly wicked grin. "Go get a towel and meet me at the jeep."

"A towel?" she raised her eyes to his questioningly.

"A towel. Now, go on!"

It took more than an hour to reach their destination, an hour in which Rory grew more and more impatient to know this private secret of Eric's.

"Here we are!" he exclaimed at last. She wondered where the surprise was as she examined the spot. It was a niche by the river, right off the main road, with beds of delicate wild violets growing to the water's edge, and a forest of trees and wild shrubbery on either bank, very beautiful but identical to much of the scenery she'd already seen.

"Hot springs!" he informed her triumphantly.

"Hot springs?" she called out after him, as he jumped out, ran around the front of the jeep, and gallantly assisted her out.

He smiled warmly as he took her hand and led her to the water's edge, explaining as they walked. "You see, at one time the Yukon was a land of volcanoes; now there are none. But we've inherited the legacy of these fantastic explosions—the small black stones mixing with white ones on the riverbanks, the smoky soil, the basalt cliffs, even the distinctive coned shape of many of the mountains. And—voilà! The hot springs!"

"Hot springs?" she repeated incredulously.

Drawing her down to her knees beside him, he submerged her hand in the water.

"Hot springs!" her eyes widened in appreciative understanding, and she laughed aloud at the pleasure of the water's warmth.

"I thought you'd never get it," he muttered playfully, as he began to unbutton his jacket. "It may be a bit chilly until we get in—"

"What are you doing?" she cried in sudden alarm, as his jacket hit the ground and he began to unbutton his shirt.

"Bathing."

"You can't be serious . . ." she began, though instinctively she knew very well that he was.

"You, I understand, had a nice warm bath yesterday." So he'd been talking to Daniel, she mused. "But I have not had that pleasure for days. I've even brought some soap!" Tremendously proud of himself, he reached into his pocket and held up a large bar of soap.

Rory was too shocked to move. He was really going to bathe, right here in front of her, with no thought of propriety. Then she caught herself. Propriety! Hadn't she always been the immodest one, the very first to throw that propriety to the wind at midnight pool parties where nude bathing had been the rage? Hadn't she nonchalantly discarded her clothes that night in the cabin? Now, she was worried about propriety. Or was she merely frightened of Eric . . . and herself?

"Aw, Rory," Eric teased. "Don't be a party pooper! You can't be *that* modest. You weren't once. And, after all, you and Daniel—"

She interrupted him nervously. "I have to tell you—"

"No. Now I am having a lovely, hot bath. Either you can stand there and watch me or you can come in and join me . . . it's your choice." Rory's eyes stubbornly held to his as her peripheral vision took in the tanned expanse of chest, then saw his hand release his belt buckle and move to the zipper of his jeans. Frantically, she turned away, as she tried to blot out the sound of denim passing over skin, the rustle of the material as it fell to the ground, then the ripple of water as he submerged himself into the hot spring.

Inwardly, Rory fumed at herself for her childish reaction. The day had been so lovely . . . until she had put this damper on it with her unfathomable primness. She had tried to tell him about her brother, yet he had denied her and she had yielded. Now, when she wanted so to join him—and she couldn't deny that both the water and Eric tempted her sorely—it was she who denied herself. Well, she decided belatedly, she was not going to be the one to mar the lovely freedom of this, a day that would have to live with her for many a long and lonely one.

"Oh, I'm coming in too!" she cried out, as she quickly began to undress, well aware that two keen eyes would be watching. Only her shirt and underwear remained when she dared to look up. Eric was, as she had suspected, following her every move, protectively covered himself by the swirling waters about his neck.

"Hurry! You'll catch cold!" he urged, though she immediately noticed that he was not taunting her. Rather, he was exhibiting the changed attitude which she had pondered earlier. Suddenly, she was no longer shy. Whether by dint of the gentleness of his voice or that uniquely special something in his glance, she no longer felt embarrassed, guilty, or depraved. Confidently, she unbuttoned her shirt and drew it off, released the clasp of her bra and did likewise, then, in a last moment's hesitation, looked once more at Eric. The strong hand extended to her erased any lingering doubts, and she stepped out of her panties and joined him in the water.

It was well worth any soul-searching she might have had to do on the bank. The water was delight-fully hot and swirling, a pure and natural whirlpool. It was, for Rory, a blue ribbon, a trophy, a diploma for having spent the past few days in this hard and demanding land. Aching muscles were soothed miraculously. Chills that had accumulated over cold ground, colder rocks, and a huge sheet of glacial ice were obliterated in the therapeutic eddy.

"Glad you joined me?" Eric asked, as if her smiles and ecstatic gurgles hadn't already given him his answer.

"You know it!" she exclaimed gleefully. "This is unbelievable!" Impulsively, she threw her arms around his neck and grinned playfully at him.

"So are you!" he murmured, as his steely arms encircled her waist and drew her body, soft, warm, and pliant, against his. She gasped involuntarily, all playfulness vanishing, as she felt his every line, every muscle, every contour come to her in the most heav-enly therapy of all.

"Eric," she whispered breathlessly, as his lips cap-tured hers, teasing and tasting, coaxing and caress-ing. Her body floated against his, her full breasts swelling against his hairy chest, her stomach fusing electrically with his, their legs twined and indistin-guishable. As the water pulsated around them, their hearts pounded in thunderous echo.

His hands began a sensual journey, touching her in spots she had never known existed but would never, from this moment on, forget. Far from dulling her awareness of them on her breasts, her hips, her thighs, the water's motion enhanced it, fueling a fire within her that sparked to her every nerve end.

His breathing was ragged when he finally released

her lips. "Do you have any idea what I'd like to do, Rory?" he asked, amber beams penetrating her very heart and soul. Weakened by his passionate assault, she merely shook her head, her hands clasped firmly against the nape of his neck. "I'd like to make love to you . . . here and now." He bent his head to nibble at her earlobe.

One part of Rory would have liked nothing better. That part was drugged by his charm and aroused by his sensuality. That part of her ached to explore the far reaches of her womanhood, to know the far reaches of his manhood. That part of her was tormented by the need to know what it would be like to be possessed, completely, by this man. That part of her begged to give herself to him, only to him.

But there was another part. This part reminded her of the none too distant hatred, disdain, and humiliation. This part reminded her of a bride named Donna, a face in a photograph that was too familiar for comfort. This part reminded her of a deception too long practiced. This part reminded her that she was . . . a virgin.

"No, Eric! I can't!" she cried, agonized by her decision.

"Oh, honey, I want you so badly!" he pleaded, and she knew all too well the truth of his words.

"No, please, Eric—" She pushed herself away from him, close to tears, and swam to shore. Hurriedly she waded out of the water, knowing that her resolve could so easily crumble, should Eric set his mind to it. But he did not. She had already dried herself and put on her underwear when she heard the water ripple and saw, out of the corner of her eye, the tall, well-muscled form, toweling himself several feet away.

"Grow up, Rory!" he muttered angrily. She remained silent, not knowing what to say, not knowing how to face his anger. As she struggled with her own emotions as well as his, he looked at her intently, his lips drawn thin when he spoke. "Sooner or later you'll have to face it, you know! It's called sexual attraction and it's a raw fact of life. My god, you act like some prim little virgin!"

"But I—" she began, only to be interrupted by his burgeoning fury.

"Don't give me your baloney! Don't tell me you don't want me just as much as I want you, because I won't believe it! You can't simply turn on and off to a man like you do . . . or look at a man, the way you're doing now . . . without desire!" Only when he had spoken the words did she realize where her eyes had wandered, and she ashamedly jerked them back to meet his once more. "Look as much as you want, little vixen. Does your Daniel look all that different . . . or doesn't he let you look at all?" he taunted.

"I'm not—"

"Save your breath! I shouldn't have asked that," he muttered. Then, as he began to dress, he spoke with a fierceness that ripped her apart. "That Daniel is a hell of a good fellow, from what I can see. How he ever got saddled with you, I'll never know! There have been times, more than one or two, when, had I pushed it, you would have been unfaithful to him . . . and loved every minute of it!"

Rory began to tremble before the onslaught. She stared in shock at the hateful outburst and his low, low opinion of her. Tears of anguish welled at her eyelids, even as the knot in her throat ruled out speech.

"You can save your tears, too," he seethed. "Some poor moron may fall for them. Not me!"

In desperation, Rory tried one more time. "Eric, let me explain—"

"I don't want to hear your explanations. I honestly don't think you have any rational ones. You're a spoiled little girl who's always had her way. Maybe Daniel pampers you and that keeps you happy. But for how long?" He was nearly yelling now, angrily buttoning his shirt as he did so. "There's more to life than that, Rory. So much more . . . but then, you wouldn't understand, would you?" His voice had lowered at the end, taking on a quality of defeat that shattered her. Now the tears were flowing down her cheeks unchecked. If this memorable day had scaled the heights, it had also plummeted to unfathomable depths.

"I told you once that I was neither a rapist nor a seducer of the undesirous. I am also a man of my word. I won't come near you again, Rory." His eyes shot amber daggers at her, spearing her anew with each word. "At some point you may understand what I've been trying to say. At some point you may see what you're missing. At that point, *you* come to *me*. But, so help me, if you demolish as decent a person as Daniel in the wake of your juvenile ignorance, I'll slam the door in your pretty face! Now, get dressed and let's go." He pivoted abruptly and stormed back to the jeep, leaving her to dress in her own private hell.

nine

BUT THE NIGHTMARE HAD JUST BEGUN. AS THE two rode back to the campsite, not a word was spoken, the air heavy, the tension nearly tangible. So distraught was Rory that she did not notice the RCMP cars that sped by them. She didn't even wonder when they reached the camp to find the same cruisers parked by the large tent, the Mounties now engaged in sober discussion with Christopher. It was only when the latter raced toward them and Eric murmured a hurried, "My God, something's happened!" as he leaped out of the jeep, that she came to her senses.

Quickly she climbed out and ran to Christopher and Eric. She raised questioning eyes to the bespectacled statesman. The latter looked cautiously at Eric before he directed his attention to Rory.

"There's been an accident," he told her quietly. Her eyes opened even wider in fear. "It's Daniel—" His voice broke off as her face went ashen, and she grabbed his arms for support.

"Is he all right?" she cried.

"We don't know, Rory," he explained calmly. "We can't get to him."

"W-where is he?" she stammered.

"He's fallen into a ravine—"

"What happened?" she interrupted.

"He fell. A ledge collapsed . . ."

Rory stiffened, remembering her own fright on a ledge earlier that very day. Only then did she look at Eric, who in turn was watching her every response with an alert eye. Not anger; she breathed a sigh of relief. Please, not anger, not now, when I need his strength, she prayed silently. Then she turned again to Christopher. "How do we get to him?" Her lower lip had begun to tremble, and she bit it to gain that small semblance of control.

"I'm just waiting for more help. The Mounties will bring additional equipment, then we can go up. It's too difficult for a helicopter. We'll have to go in on foot."

"I-is he moving?" she whispered, afraid to express her fears more directly.

Slowly and reluctantly, Christopher shook his head. This time Rory's knees did buckle, but it was Eric whose firm arm around her waist kept her from falling. "It doesn't mean anything, Rory." He attempted to reassure her, his voice soft and calm. "He may just know enough not to move until help arrives. We can't assume the worst."

"Eric's right," Christopher joined in. "Let's not jump to any conclusions until we know something more definite."

"How long until the rescue team gets here?" Eric asked, having taken over the questioning from Rory, who had lapsed into a state of stunned silence.

Again Christopher shrugged. "Should be any time now . . . that may be them now." He pointed toward the road where the slowly rising crescendo of tires on gravel announced the arrival of the rescue van. It ground to a halt and six more men clambered out. Eric and Christopher immediately moved to greet them.

Rory looked around frantically, feeling suddenly alone and lost. In that instant she realized exactly how much she had relied on Daniel for stability. Even during those stretches when he had been away on assignment, he had been the backbone of the family. Now there was a chance that the backbone was seriously injured. . . .

In the grip of despair, she sank down on a nearby boulder. Through fearful eyes, she watched the circle of men, some gesturing, others pointing, all deeply involved in the tragic drama. Whether this turn of events would have been as devastating, had it not happened simultaneously with her falling out with Eric, Rory had no way of knowing. She was only aware of a mammoth void deep within her, of the sense of her very world having collapsed irretrievably.

She became conscious of Eric separating from the group and approaching her, and numbly she rose to meet him. His eyes were chilling though his tone was even. "We'll be leaving as soon as we can load up. You are to stay here—"

"No! I have to come with you."

"You can't come." His expression was forbidding.

"There's got to be something I can do. . . ." she pleaded in desperation, her eyes shimmering with tears.

He took her shoulders firmly. "No. You will only slow us down. You've already made the trek out and back once today. Stay here. Daniel will need you in reasonable condition when we get him back." She didn't argue, yet there was something in her eyes, other than the welling tears, which caught his attention. "Will you be all right here alone?" he asked more quietly, only the barest trace of past tenderness in his voice.

She nodded. How could she explain the sense of desolation that engulfed her? He had asked if she would be all right alone; she knew she had no choice! The last thing she could do was to beg him to stay with her, yet it was the first thing she wanted! How could he hate her so? The coldness in his eyes, the harshness of his fingers on her shoulders . . . in utter defeat, she bowed her head and turned away, returning to her rocky perch to watch the proceedings, helpless and dazed.

Within minutes, the camp was emptied of all signs of life, save the occasional unconscious fidgeting of the petite, sandy-haired girl clad in sneakers, blue jeans, and plaid jacket. Rory kept her eyes on the path the men had taken, while her mind replayed a lifetime of her brother's love and support and guidance. She conjured up images of good times and bad, of reward and punishment, of success and failure. Daniel had always been there when she needed him, yet here she sat, drained and helpless, an aeon away from where he now lay, hurt and alone, awaiting help.

It was with a feeling of betrayal that her mind strayed to the other major player in the drama of her life, one who had just recently arrived on the stage. She loved him hopelessly. The ache within her at his disaffection was nearly as great as the tormenting uncertainty about her brother's fate.

With the exception of that traumatic day, so long ago, when her father had left the family, Rory's life had been a steady progression of highs, shallow perhaps, but buoyant nonetheless. She had seemingly been on top of the world, until she had first seen that faint surface crack, pointed out so indirectly at first by the Dwyers, which had inspired this search for greater meaning. The fissure had widened the more she searched, shattering open a Pandora's box of fears and insecurities, roadblocks and challenges.

Now, as she sat on the cold hard stone, silently watching and waiting as the sun moved steadily west, she shuddered at the extent to which her peace had been fractured, both by her own doings and by the hand of fate. The future was suddenly an obscure no man's land. She faced a terrifying reality, she who had always known security. She knew somehow that she was confronting the greatest test and that she would emerge with a new and long-sought inner strength . . . or be broken.

Thoughts of supper never entered her mind, as the red rays of sunset yielded to the purples of dusk, wrapping the camp, and worse, the mountain, in a deep mist of gloom. Rory looked at her watch nervously. The rescue team had to have reached the site long since, yet she was unable to even guess when they would return. Surely they had searchlights and would continue their work in the darkness. But the going would be slower, and even Rory's inexperienced mind told her that each passing hour without the appropriate medical care would lessen Daniel's chances of survival.

Out of desperation, she built up a blazing fire, its warmth only reminding her by comparison how cold the mountainside could be. The air was still, rent only by the gentle sounds of the wild—the hooting of the night owl, the distant flow of the river, the crackle of dry logs in the blaze. In vain she listened for the sound of human footsteps returning over the hilly path with a precious burden.

Minutes flowed into hours. Another log was added, then another. The rising sparks provided the only light, yet Rory prayed to the moon to cast its glow on the other side of the mountain, where the need for light was greater than hers. Slowly and painfully, the night dragged on. Her whole being agonized for lack of word, beset by panicky images of a critically injured brother, out of reach of all help or relief. Her every muscle tensed in anticipation. But the waiting . . . the waiting . . .

Suddenly her head jerked up, ears and eyes instantly alert to a faint sound from the distant mountainside. As it drew steadily closer, she heard voices and knew that the waiting had ended. In its place came a terror, a pure terror of finding out whether or not her brother had been reached in time. To sit and wait and wonder was one thing; to find oneself on the verge of a traumatic or a relieving discovery was another.

As the small army neared, she ran to the edge of the camp, just in time to see the first floodlight beam around the curve. Jumping aside to yield to the hurrying men, she watched wide-eyed and mute as the stretcher carrying her brother came into view, approached, then passed her on its way to the rescue truck. She could neither speak nor move, but merely stood paralyzed in the darkness.

She might have remained behind, unseen by the Mounties, had it not been for Christopher's gentle but firm arm around her waist, leading her quickly toward the wagon and the stretcher. "He's alive." He spoke confidently to her, only he knowing the true nature of her feelings for the injured man. "We'll take him to the hospital in Whitehorse and then have him transferred in the morning, if necessary. You can ride with him, if you'd like."

Rory said nothing as she was helped into the truck and shown to a seat by Daniel's side. Swallowing hard, she looked down, in the dim light of the truck, into his face, ghostly pale and still; timidly, she reached out and took his hand, praying that hers could warm his cold, limp one. As the truck's motor came to life and began to move, the specially trained medical technicians worked—probing, wrapping, connecting intravenous tubes, consulting one another in hushed tones. It was only when the activity seemed to die down that Rory finally found the courage to question them.

"What's the matter with him?" she haltingly asked of the medic, who seemed to be in charge.

The man looked up from his patient, as though seeing her for the first time. "Hard to tell exactly, ma'am. 'Til we get 'im to the hospital." Then, at her beseeching expression, he added, "Looks like multiple fractures and possible spinal damage. Some internal injuries . . . hard to tell. It's the unconsciousness that worries me most." He rubbed his forehead as he looked back at Daniel.

"H-has he been conscious at all since you found him?" she asked, her voice quavering dangerously.

"Not yet."

The hard, blunt edge of reality sent shock waves of renewed terror through her. She was infinitely grateful for Christopher's comforting arm, which fell across her shoulder, though she hadn't previously been aware of him beside her. She looked around at the band of strange faces and then back at that sympathetic one.

"Will he live, Christopher?" she whispered weakly.

Her guardian angel smiled the most encouraging smile he could muster. "We hope so, Rory. Just think about getting him to the hospital. One thing at a time."

She nodded in agreement, the steady drone of the motor mercifully preventing her from catching the frequently dismal conversation between the medics. Christopher's presence was reassuring, and gradually she felt her trembling muscles begin to quiet. Only then did she venture more questions.

"How did the accident happen, Christopher? Daniel was so adept at—"

"It wasn't his fault," he explained sympathetically. "Unfortunately, tragedies happen. Not to sound trite, he was in the wrong place at the wrong time. He was on that ledge taking pictures when the tremor hit. It was too thin to hold together and simply collapsed.

"Tremor?"

"There was a very slight movement of the rock this afternoon—nothing significant, had it not been for Dan's accident."

A puzzled look crossed her features. "We didn't feel any tremor. . . ." she began.

"You and Eric were too far away at the time." There was no criticism in his tone, and Rory nodded in understanding. Then, for the first conscious moment since Daniel had been brought from the mountain, she allowed herself to think of her nemesis. Her voice was meek when she finally found the strength to ask.

"Where is Eric now?"

Christopher gave her an added hug, sensing her need. "He's following us in the jeep. He'll meet us at the hospital."

Rory wasn't sure whether to be relieved or not at this news. On the one hand, she wanted him to comfort her, to hold her, to tell her that everything would be all right. On the other hand, she knew that he would not and that she was going to have to learn to stand on her own two feet. Christopher would help her for now. Then, perhaps when Daniel was better . . .

But the outlook for Daniel's recovery was grim. He was whisked away at the door of the Emergency Unit when the long ride was over. She was ushered into a small waiting room. More waiting . . . uselessness . . . helplessness . . . She looked out the window into the darkness at a world quiet and asleep. Could it be that a flurry of lifesaving activity was indeed taking place down the hall . . . or was it all a mockery. Did Daniel have a fighting chance?

"Coffee?" She recognized the deep voice without raising her eyes, and gratefully reached for the styrofoam cup. She was aware of his taking a seat, though she made no attempt at conversation. Once she dared to look up and her gaze locked with unfathomable amber orbs that studied her relentlessly. She doubted if she had the strength to tear her eyes away when Christopher arrived.

"Any word?" he asked softly, sitting down and taking her free hand in his. She grimaced as she shook her head. Questioningly, he looked at Eric.

"He's on the operating table. It'll be awhile yet."

Once more Christopher turned to Rory. "Can I get

you anything?" Again, she shook her head. "Let me know if you change your mind, okay?"

Green eyes, drowning in worry, focused on him as she attempted to explain. "I can't . . ." she whispered, before her throat constricted, cutting off all further speech.

"Just try to take it easy." He patted her hand in his uniquely paternal way. "They're doing everything they can. . . ."

"I know," she mouthed as she stood up. Behind her, Christopher moved next to Eric, and the two sat talking in muted voices, leaving her to wallow in her personal misery.

She looked at her watch once, then again but three minutes later. She glanced toward the hallway for signs of movement and, seeing none, turned her gaze back to the night. Her eyes were drawn to the lighted waiting room's reflection in the window, to the reflection of the two men, heads close together, finally to the image of Eric, as dark in his seat as the blackness outside. His hair and beard blended with the night, but his hands gleamed from out of the darkness, very much as she had painted them in her memory. Lean though strong, gentle yet hard, still uncallused, she recalled their play about her face, her neck, her body. How she longed to have them playing about her now, comforting her, pleasuring her, coaxing her to forget the unfolding tragedy, if only for a few precious minutes. His head turned toward the window and met her gaze, briefly and electrically; quickly she jerked hers away, castigating herself mercilessly for harboring such selfish and wanton thoughts at such a time as this.

Furious with herself, she turned and rushed out of the waiting room, her sneakers squeaking noisily on the linoleum as she headed for the nurses' station. "Is there any word yet on Daniel Turner?" she softly begged the nurse on duty.

Cool and impersonal, the nurse sent her a look of impatience. "I believe you were told that the doctor would be in to see you as soon as he is done. You'd be best to wait in there—" As she pointed back toward the waiting room, Rory interrupted.

"But I *have* been waiting and now I'd like to know what's happening in there!" she exclaimed, her voice rising steadily. She was trying desperately to keep calm, but the waiting was gradually taking its toll. Always the waiting . . .

"I'm sorry, miss. There's nothing I can do." The nurse dismissed her curtly and turned back to her work.

"But, surely—" Rory began hysterically.

"Come on, Rory." It was Eric, taking her by the shoulders and guiding her beside him. She peered anxiously at his face, so far above hers, and was surprised to see that a gentleness had returned to his features and that he spoke to her softly. "There's no point in working yourself up. We can only wait." He led her back to her seat in the waiting room, then sat down beside her. Christopher was there still, seemingly lost in his own thoughts.

Rory curled her legs beneath her and wrapped her arms around her stomach, as though to thereby comfort herself. When it failed to help, she looked hesitantly at Eric. "Did any of the others come in with you?"

He nodded. "Tony is here. He's been trying to get through to his publisher. He is taking this very badly. Seems to feel it is his fault." He looked sideways at her for reaction to his words.

"*His* fault? How could it have been anyone's fault? No one planned that tremor!" she exclaimed.

Eric sighed. "He feels that it should have been him up on that ledge . . . in the ravine . . . on that operating table right now. After all, he was the photographer. It was his job to take those pictures, not Daniel's!"

"How can you be so heartless?" she lashed out at him, this time drawing Christopher's head up in surprise. "Tony is terrified of heights. He should never have been here in the first place! And I'm sure he would have had fantastic pictures even without the one from the ledge. . . ." Her voice cracked on the last word, and she struggled to keep her composure.

"Shhh. I agree with you," Eric crooned, taking her clenched fist between his hands. "I'm only telling you what *he* is feeling, about now. He's taking the whole thing out on himself." Gently Eric's fingers massaged her fist, coaxing it into relaxation, extending her fingers one by one until he could feel the tension begin to ease.

"He shouldn't do that," she whispered finally, savoring the comfort of Eric's touch. It was, she knew, the only food she really needed to sustain her through the ordeal.

"It might help if you tell him that," he suggested quietly. Rory looked at him again, unconsciously moving from one to the other of his beloved features. He was, she thought, not only the most handsome man she had known, but also the most sensible and considerate, when he wanted to be. If only . . . if only . . .

She tore her gaze away, embarrassed at the promiscuity of her gaze. Her eyes could say so much more than she would allow her tongue to do. How much did he suspect of her true feelings, she wondered. He seemed so quick to read her thoughts. Was she as transparent on this issue as well?

Then she chided herself. What difference did it make, after all, if he knew that she had fallen in love with him? He despised her and would be indifferent to her feelings. But what a laugh he would have, what fuel for mockery these, her most inner thoughts, would give him! For that reason alone, she could never tell him how much she loved him!

The vigil was interminable. Eric stayed by Rory's side, though she kept her hands in her lap. Periodically, the agony of the wait brought a moan to her lips, and at each of these times he reached out to comfort her; each time she withdrew to herself, refusing his gesture as subtly as possible. Finally, before dawn, she crumbled, yielding helplessly to the silent tears which had been threatening all night. This time, when he put a protective arm about her shoulder, she melted against him more needful of the tender comfort he offered than mindful of the emotional implications.

The gray light of dawn was at the window when a weary-eyed surgeon finally appeared at the door. Three heads simultaneously jerked in his direction, and Rory bolted up, her heart in her throat. Her rounded eyes asked the questions which her choked voice could not. The surgeon looked from one to the other of the three before settling on Rory as the primary party involved. His gaze was direct, his tone sober.

"He's in the recovery room," he began. "I'm afraid his condition is critical." Rory flinched at his choice of words, and her knees trembled. She was only marginally aware of Eric, placing his hands on her arms to support her. Grimly, the doctor continued. "We've stopped the internal bleeding, but the back and neck injuries are serious. He doesn't seem to be responding at this point."

"Can I see him?" she whispered timidly.

"Not quite yet, I'm afraid. He'll be taken to the Intensive Care Unit in another hour or two. Then you'll be able to see him."

Dazed, Rory managed to turn and walk away from the doctor, leaving Christopher to ask for the details which she was unable to fathom. Eric took her elbow and guided her back to her chair, then with a gentle, "Wait here," he too joined the surgeon.

Rory sat with her elbows on her knees, her face buried in her hands. She hadn't slept in almost twenty-four hours, yet she wasn't tired. She hadn't eaten since lunch the day before, yet she wasn't hungry. She was numb, dazed, in a state of bewilderment.

And the waiting continued. She passed through some periods when she felt better, some when she started to tremble anew. During one of the former, she found a ladies' room and washed her face and hands, combed her hair, and put on a pale lipstick and blusher, shocked by the ashen face that stared back at her from the mirror.

True to his word, the doctor returned an hour and a half later, freshly shaven and dressed in ordinary clothes, to announce that his patient had been placed in the ICU and that Rory could see him. Eric and Christopher walked with her to the room, then waited outside the glass windows as she timidly approached the bed.

Rory's heart lurched when she saw his face still with the same ghostly pallor. Again, she took his hand; again, it was cold and limp. "Has he regained consciousness at all?"

The doctor shook his head.

"What are his chances?" she whispered, not for an instant taking her liquid gaze from her brother's face.

"Truthfully?" He paused. "Not very good," he finally replied. Although Rory knew that he had tried to be as gentle as his objectivity permitted, she cringed at his words.

"May I stay here?" she asked, only then turning pleading eyes to those of the doctor. "Please?" she begged in a hoarse whisper, the agony of the last hours of waiting written over her every feature.

"Well." He hesitated, looking once more at his patient before continuing. "I suppose you can, though you really could use some rest yourself. If that young man of yours awakes and sees you looking like death warmed over . . ." But Rory's interest had quickly gone from his words. Silently, she drew up a chair and, taking Daniel's hand in hers again, sat down by his bed, determined to be there when he did finally awaken.

The determination stayed with her throughout the day, though there was not the slightest flicker to indicate that Daniel knew she was there. At Christopher's insistence, she went through the motions of eating something for lunch, in the end leaving more of the sandwich in its soggy paper wrapper than in her stomach. Her thoughts focused on her brother, willing him to look at her, speak to her, at least hear her as she spoke his name repeatedly.

Nothing. She was aware of the movement of others, periodically Eric or Christopher, outside the

glass walls of the room. She watched as the doctors
and nurses came to examine their patient. She shifted
stiffly in her seat as the light of afternoon became the
evening sunset. Yet from her brother, nothing.

Darkness had fallen once again when Eric
returned, insisting—against her vehement protest—
that she join them for dinner. Again, no hunger. She
resisted anew when Eric led her bodily from the
restaurant to the nearby inn.

"I've taken some rooms, Rory. You've got to get
some sleep," he explained, as he took two sets of
keys from the clerk, tossing a third to Christopher.

She held back stubbornly. "But I have to get back
to the hospital," she argued, only vaguely aware of
the hour or the reality of Daniel's condition.

"Rory." He spoke as if to a child. "Daniel is asleep
for the night. And you will collapse if you keep this
up." She was alert enough to notice the lines of
fatigue around his own eyes, the grim set of his
mouth, the disheveled look to his hair, as though he
had run his fingers through it repeatedly.

Doggedly she persisted. "What if he wakes up? I
want to *be* there!"

His arm was around her shoulder, propelling her
toward the stairs of the inn. He spoke softly yet confidently. "The doctors know where you are. I informed
the nurses' station, also. They will call immediately if
there is any change."

Whether it was the sureness of his tone or the
actual words, something deep inside knew he was
right. Obediently, she let herself be led up the stairs,
down a hallway, and into a small room with a large
feather bed.

Immediately, she walked to the edge of the bed
and sat down, her eyes glued to the floor, her fingers

clutching the faded green cotton bedspread. Eric remained at the door for several moments, hands folded across his chest, waiting for some intelligible movement from her. He was perplexed at the way she had fallen apart. She had been such a tough, spunky sort, yet she now seemed totally vulnerable. For a self-centered young lady, she was unusually engrossed in the welfare of another, and for that instant, he envied Daniel more than anyone else in the world, for the strength of the feeling this petite spitfire held for him. Why the two, Daniel and Rory, had not married was a mystery to him! If his own marriage had only had such feeling . . .

When the small figure on the bed remained motionless, he approached her, kneeling down to search her downcast eyes. "Rory," he began, with a pleading tone she had only heard once before, on that fateful yesterday, now light years ago, "you've got to pull yourself together. If you love Daniel, do it for him. He would not want to see you like this. Do you understand what I'm saying?"

This pleading tone snapped her out of her lethargy. "Yes," she whispered.

He continued to coax her, in a near whisper himself. "Good. Now, I want you to take a nice, hot bath and then go to bed. I will be right across the hall. Chris is two doors down. If you need either of us, we'll be there. I have instructed the clerk to get all three of us immediately if the hospital calls. Understand?"

She nodded, a forced smile the only means she had of saying thank you for the comfort which he had—to his own great discomfort, she felt convinced—given her. She watched as he walked to the door, turned to look at her once more, then left.

His words became the major logical force working in her beleaguered brain. "Take a nice, hot bath," he had said. So she took a nice, hot bath. As she soaked, her fevered mind vacillated between images of Daniel's cold, limp hand and Eric's warm, reassuring one, the first swamping her with fear, the second with guilt.

She remembered the only peaceful moments she'd had during the past twenty-four hours, when, in the hospital waiting room, she had sought a haven within the circle of Eric's arms. He had, for those moments, absorbed her pain and dulled the ache of worry and fear that had gnawed at her unremittingly since she first learned of Daniel's accident. Unbeknownst to him, she had fallen even more deeply in love with him in those few moments. It was an addiction which she knew she would have to kick, but she couldn't do it now. Maybe tomorrow. Next week. Next year. But not now! She needed him so badly! Certainly Daniel would not begrudge her thoughts of Eric on this difficult night. For, as unrealistic as her love for him was, it was all she had.

She watched the water swirl down the drain before she stood and dried herself off. "And then go to bed," he had told her; diligently, she did so. For lack of any nightwear, she crawled bareskinned between the sheets, a heavy quilt bringing whatever warmth her tired body needed.

There she lay, waiting for the blessing of sleep to free her, albeit temporarily, from her torment. But this was to be a new game of waiting, the cruelest and most agonizing yet. For, exhausted as she was, her mind replayed the recent happenings again and again, inevitably focusing on Daniel's inert features, so still and frightening. It was like a recurring nightmare, worsening with every toss and turn.

At the slightest sound in the hallway, she bolted upright, her heart thudding in anticipation of a knock on the door. Alternately relieved and disappointed, hopeful and desolate, she curled into a ball of tension, alone and isolated. Once before, not so many nights ago, she had lain thus, eventually to be comforted so sweetly. . . .

This time she was alone. When the tears came, there was no one to hug her, to warm her, to whisper words of reassurance in her ear. She felt the loss of that presence more intensely than anything else. If only Eric would help her, one last time. She needed him, she wanted him, she doubted whether she could make it until morning without him.

Driven by a most basic and primitive force, she climbed out of bed and drew on her jeans and sweater. Tears were still wet on her cheeks when she crossed the hallway, her need increasing with every step. She hesitated but once before she knocked softly on his door, her urgent need far outweighing the fear of his rejection.

The door opened, then widened in silent invitation. She walked softly past him into the room, turning only when she heard the click behind her. The room was lit by a single lamp on the small coffee table. The bed was rumpled, though unslept in. Her eyes met Eric's as he leaned back against the door. He was dressed as he had been on that other night, in the deserted cabin, stripped to the waist and barefooted, as was she, with only tight, faded blue jeans to break the devastating expanse of his skin.

As she stared at him wordlessly, she saw the weariness in his face and a pain that matched her own. For a heart-stopping moment, she anticipated a renewal of his last angry tirade at the hot springs.

"*You* come to *me*," he had said. And she had. Emotion choked her voice, yet he waited for her to say something, mindful of the tears she'd shed, heedful of others on the way. She swallowed once, then again, as her mind groped for the right words. She wanted desperately to tell him about Daniel. She wanted desperately to tell him about herself. Most of all, she wanted desperately to tell him about himself, and the awesome love he had inspired.

His figure blurred in her vision as tears of anguish burst forth. A new wave of loneliness and fear rose from her depths, and she could think of nothing but the dire necessity of his strong arms about her.

"I need you." It was barely a whisper, broken by a sob, yet Eric heard it. She repeated it, now crying aloud in a tone of utter agony. "I need you. . . ." She wanted to run to him, yet that lingering fear of rejection kept her bare feet glued to the hardwood floor. Eric stood still, his expression of uncertainty unseen through her tears. She hunched her shoulders and lowered her head, her body quaking under the pressure of her sobs.

As she neared the deepest point of despair, his arms encircled her shoulders and drew her against him. Her trembling prevented her from feeling the tremor that passed through him as she wrapped her arms around his neck and buried her face in his neck.

"Why did you wait so long?" he murmured against her hair, as he bent, lifted her into his arms, and carried her to the bed. There, he sank down, cradling her in his lap, rocking her back and forth, as she cried out the fear and heartbreak within her soul. She felt the warmth and strength of his body reach out to her, and she drank in all he offered. It was only when the tears slowed and the trembling ceased that she held her head back to look into his face. It was soft and gentle and everything she had hoped it would be. As angry as he had been with her in the past, he had come through for her now.

Amber eyes roamed her face, their flames sending a new message, one which Rory now understood. "I need you," she murmured breathlessly, one last time. His hands came up to frame her small face, his lips down to kiss away the last remnants of tears from her eyes and cheeks. Then, the sensual cleanup complete, his lips skimmed down to her mouth, where her parted lips waited. It was a slow and extended interplay, their mouths exploring one another's, his tongue seeking hers out in a fiercely gentle probing.

Contrary to the urgency of Rory's need, Eric deliberately set a lazy pace, allowing a thoroughness at every spot that was guaranteed to drive away the pain and misery that beseiged her. She did not know when comfort turned to stimulation, so masterful was his seduction, yet she found herself climbing higher and higher with every lick of his tongue, nip of his teeth, touch of his lips. She sighed at this new torment, so sweet and heady, the ache inside now physical and in her most private and unknown parts.

One after the other, he administered long, drugging kisses as his hands joined the play, caressing her neck, shoulders, and back, then moving beneath her sweater to cut her ripe breasts, creamy soft and swelling. Her hands raked lightly through the manly mat of hair on his chest, reveling in the strength of rippling muscles, delighting in the feel of taut flesh.

He took the bottom of her sweater and gently pulled it up over her head, discarding it carelessly as his eyes devoured the richness of her ivory skin and

the pink firmness of her erotic buds. Ever so tenderly, as though handling a porcelain doll, he lay her
down on the bed, spreading her arms to her sides as
he admired her anew.

"You are so beautiful," he rasped huskily. Slowly
his lips descended to tantalize her breasts and she
moaned in delight as his tongue teased their rising
crests to pebble-hardness. Then he eased his body
half atop hers as his lips seared a path of passion
from her breasts to her chest and throat, nibbling on
her chin before capturing her mouth once again.

The fire within her had come to life, sparking in
her loins and flaming upward, flaring higher with
each kiss and every caress. She felt a simultaneous
urgency in him, a need he could neither hide nor
deny. In a burst of emotion, he grabbed her to him,
crushing her breasts against his chest, her own arms
clutching his broad back fervently.

They had passed into a new phase of passion. Each
recognized it, each welcomed it eagerly. One final
time, Eric held her back from him, his eyes caressing
her body, then rising to meet her excited gaze.

"Let me make love to you. Let me pleasure you." It
was more of a question than she had expected. He
was giving her a chance to change her mind. But she
knew what she wanted; there would be no turning
back. She craved him, she ached for him, she needed
him. Above all, she loved him and wanted to give him
her very own, unique something. In answer to his
question, she moved her hands to the nape of his
neck and drew his head down to meet her parted
lips, their sensual movement giving him all the
answer he wanted.

This time, when he eased her down upon the bed,
he sat up himself, his hands moving to her jeans,

unsnapping, unzipping, then drawing them off easily. He looked for a long moment at her body, slim and bare and beautiful before him, then he kissed her again while his hands began an intimate and excruciatingly arousing exploration of her femininity. The tide of passion threatened to drown her, as she moaned under the burden of restraint. Sensing the high pitch of her arousal, he moved to take off his own pants.

How different this was from the incident at the hot springs. Here, in this small inn room, they were man and woman, in their most primitive state. Slowly, Eric lowered himself on top of her, and she gasped aloud at the feel of him against her body. That he wanted her just as much as she did him was vividly clear. He rained kisses on her face, her neck, her breasts, as his body drove hers to even greater heights. His hands touched her freely, petting her abdomen, her hips, her thighs.

Rory was conscious of nothing in the world save Eric. All other thought had been forced from her mind except that of his body near hers, beside hers, on hers. She thrilled again and again at the beauty of his touch, the spiraling passion that carried her higher than she'd ever dreamed possible. She sought to beg to be totally possessed, so heated was her need, when his hips slid between her thighs and the manly boldness probed her resisting flesh. Then, in one heartrending, earth-shattering moment, he stiffened and held back, his eyes uncomprehending as they searched hers.

"Rory?" he gasped huskily, his breathing ragged, his voice unsure, his arms suddenly trembling on her either side. She, too, was taken by surprise. This was not part of the scenario; he was not supposed to know *before!* "What the . . . Rory?" He held her gaze, reading in her eyes what he had suspected. "It can't be . . . but, Daniel . . . Rory, what's going on here?"

Any satisfaction she might have had at finally rendering this most confident of men nonplussed was unnoticed. His mention of her brother's name was a veritable bucket of ice water, quenching the flames of passion. She pulled herself from beneath him, turned her back, and drew her knees up to her chest, the ache in her loins once again becoming a knot of misery.

She steeled herself for his anger, braced herself for further humiliation. But neither came. "Rory?" he repeated her name gently. He moved himself deftly around until he sat facing her on the bed. "Rory, you *are* a virgin, aren't you?"

She kept her moist eyes on the bedsheet beneath, her chin tucked firmly on her chest. He knew; the deceit was just about done. She nodded her head in misery, as her cheeks dampened with tears once more.

"But, how?" he asked incredulously. "If you and Daniel are lovers . . ." He paused, thinking aloud. Then, her greatest fear was realized, his voice hardened, chillingly. "But, you aren't lovers, are you? It's all been a lie!"

Rory shook her head without looking up, too ashamed to meet his justifiable anger. "No, I never lied." She sobbed uncontrollably.

"Then, what's this all about?" he yelled, getting up in agitation and pacing to the window, heedless of his own nakedness and hers. "Why the game, Rory? Answer me!"

It was the moment of truth, whether she liked it or not. "You frightened me, Eric," she screamed back at him, then, letting several soulful sobs out, added more quietly, "I frightened myself."

"Hah!" he exploded, his eyes flashing danger signals. "That's more like it! The little girl couldn't cope with her woman's body, so the fairy tale goes. She makes up stories—"

"No! *You* decided we were lovers. I just never denied it." She sobbed in her own defense.

His voice took on an even more harsh and infuriated tone as he stalked to the edge of the bed. "And who in the hell is Daniel? A good friend? A eunuch? Why in the devil did you chase all the way up here to see him? What did you really do in that damned tent of his?" He threw himself down upon the bed in front of her and shook her forcefully, knocking the breath from her and effectively choking off her sobs, as he demanded a final time, "just what *is* he to you?"

Rory crumbled in the face of his violent outburst, her every bone, muscle, and nerve end crying out in defeat. "He's my brother," she shrieked, then repeated the long overdue truth in a mere whisper. "My brother." Tears coursed down her cheeks as she wept silently, beneath Eric's rigid features. There was a long and agonized silence, during which she imagined the further hatred her deception was sure to inspire. Finally, he spoke, hesitant and disbelieving.

"How can that be?" But rather than the hatred she expected, there came a hurt into his eyes, which shattered her all the more. As calmly as she could, she explained between spasms the discrepancy in names. He listened as calmly, but the hurt lingered. "Why didn't you tell me, for God's sake? How could you have kept it to yourself . . . through all . . . this?"

She thought the tears had all been spent, yet his

reference to Daniel's accident brought them again and with a vengeance. She shrugged through the mist. "I tried . . . the other day . . . at the hot springs. I should have told you sooner . . . I've been so stupid . . . he wanted me to tell you . . ." she whispered.

The hands on her shoulders had suddenly become gentle. "You *do* love him, don't you?" he asked, with a tenderness that provoked more tears.

She raised her head and looked at him through long, wet lashes, putting every bit of earnestness she possessed into her faltering speech. "Yes, I-I do l-love him. He's m-my brother. He's all I have in the w-world. And now he's d-dying." She looked away in abject despair. "I f-feel so lost." Her voice lowered to a whisper. "I want so to be strong . . ."

"You will be." Eric's words were immediate, clear, and full of confidence as he pulled her against him. His embrace now provided solace, conveyed an inner strength to her very marrow, which comforted her as effectively as his masterful sexual prowess had stimulated her. She listened to the beat of his heart against her ear, its steadiness a pacemaker for her own.

When he drew away from her, she clung to him, terrified at the thought of losing this sanctuary. "It's all right, honey." He reassured her with an easy smile, taking her hands from behind his back. "I just want to get our clothes."

Rory cringed fearfully. "Can't I please stay here . . . just for a little longer?" she cried, wide-eyed.

He took her face between his two strong hands. "I'm not letting you go anywhere. I want you to spend the night here with me. But I won't risk things getting out of hand the way they nearly did a little while ago." A black eyebrow arched suggestively, a subtle reminder of past mischief.

Now Rory lapsed into a state of bewilderment all
her own. She knew that Eric was merely comforting
her out of pity, that he despised her for what she was
and what she had done. She had come to him earlier
with the intention of giving herself fully to him. And
he would have taken her, when he thought she was
Daniel's lover. Yet he rejected her when he found her
to be untouched. Why? Why? Confusion was written
all over her face when he brought her clothes to her,
having already pulled on his own. Despite her confusion, she suddenly became aware of her nudity and
hurriedly dressed herself.

Eric watched her movements alertly, only
approaching her when she was done. "There's a time
and place for everything," he began quietly, placing
an iron finger beneath her chin to tilt it up toward
him. "A woman's virginity is something very special,
Rory. It should be given out of love, not out of need
or . . . despair."

"But—" she began, intent on confessing her love,
unrequited as it was.

"Shhh." He stilled her words with a finger against
her lips. "I think we could both use some rest," he
crooned gently, as he drew her into his arms and
down upon the bed, pulling the quilt over them.
"Now, sleep," he ordered her softly, as he brushed
the wayward curls from her forehead, tenderly
kissed the tip of her nose, then put his own dark
head down on the pillow.

ten

THE EARLY MORNING SEATTLE SUN FILTERED through tiny slats in the woven bamboo shade, creating a feathering play of light on Rory's slumber-graced features. Sleepily, she rolled over and reached for the watch she had left on her bedstand. It was only eight, a far cry from the noon hour she had expected for this Saturday morning, when she had neither classes to attend nor deadlines to meet.

Lazily she rolled back toward the sun, so bright and cheerful as it beckoned through the yellow shade, and sat up. Her bare feet sank into the plush lemon carpet as she padded to the window and raised the shade. Another beautiful morning . . . but then, wasn't Seattle renowned for beautiful mornings?

As she thrust her feet into her fluffy mules, she smiled in satisfaction at the decorating job she had done in her bedroom, and indeed, in the whole apartment. Neither decorator nor friend—though Monica had accompanied her on the spree—had influenced her choice of carpeting, furniture, window dressing, or accessories, and she was hence doubly proud of the results.

An apartment of her own had been a must. From the moment Daniel regained consciousness after a harrowing week-long coma, Rory had sensed that new life had been granted them both. For her brother, it was the miracle of recovery. It was a long road he faced, one of further hospitalization, weeks of recuperation, and intense physical therapy.

For Rory, it was the miracle of finding, during the endless hours of bedside vigil, when she had been forced to contemplate a future alone, that long-sought inner strength. The process that began in the congenial atmosphere of Charles and Monica's apartment and had climaxed during those eventful days in the Yukon, had finally reached fruition—ironically, at that time of crisis. The days of waiting had given time for thought. Even before Daniel awoke from his state of unconsciousness, she had begun to formulate her future.

And the logical first step, when Dan was sufficiently over the hurdle, up and about, even getting back gradually to work, was this apartment. It had everything she needed and was spacious and airy without being a monstrosity to clean. Additionally, as it turned out, it was a mere ten-minute drive to the university, where she had enrolled as a special student for the fall semester. Yes, she loved her new home, she mused, as she pulled back the blanket and sheets to air and shuffled into the bathroom to wash up.

After soaping her hands and face and brushing her teeth, she worked through the unruly mass of sandy-colored curls, studying her reflection in the mirror as she did so. Well, she thought, she looked the same as she had yesterday, but her face certainly looked different now than it had when she first moved here nearly three months ago. Then it had been gaunt and pale, wracked by the worry of those first long weeks after the accident, etched with the pain of another, equally painful trauma.

Though the second trauma was never far from her consciousness, she had finally begun to accept what she could not change. The face that looked back at her now was softer and more relaxed. A flush of pink, dabbed on her cheeks as she slept, remained to highlight her creamy smooth complexion. She had filled out in those three months, not only due to proper eating, an activity nearly forgotten in the horror of the hospital vigil, but due to the maturity which slowly and steadily, though still often painfully, had developed within to shape her appearance. It had been a long, hard period, but there seemed, indeed, to be a dawn after the night.

Setting down her hairbrush, she smiled to herself. The nightshirt she wore was perfect, its pale pink color matching her slippers and bringing out the beautiful tawny tone of her hair. An oversized football jersey she had bought on a whim, it suggested the easy relaxation she intended for a lazy day like today.

With the lightest skip to her step, she went into the kitchen to make herself the bacon and eggs she had been looking forward to all week. Amazing how easily one could adjust to cooking when one wanted to, she mused, as she put the frying pan into the sink to soak and carried her plate to the table. With coffee already perking, the only thing missing was the newspaper. Absently, she padded to the door and drew it open in search of her printed breakfast companion.

What she found made her gasp aloud in fright, then surprise. For her newspaper was not in its usual place on the doormat, but rather in the hand of a most unlikely delivery boy. She had not seen him since Daniel left the hospital, nearly four months ago, yet he had been such a fixed and vivid presence in her mind that she felt as though it had been but yesterday.

Eric, had, in fact, been close by her side following the night they'd spent so innocently together. It was an infinite comfort for her to look up from her post by Daniel's bed to find Eric nearby, waiting and watching silently, as did she. Words seemed irrelevant at the time; it had been a kind of limbo into which they'd been cast, freed by one truth only to be paralyzed by another. Then, as Daniel slowly showed signs of recovery, Eric's presence had faded, little by little, until one day, Rory emerged from her emotional maelstrom to find him gone. That had been the last she'd seen of him, standing beside her as she talked with Daniel, telling him of all he'd missed during his prolonged sleep.

It was only when she'd become fully convinced that her brother would, indeed, recover that she'd permitted herself to ponder her own aches and pains, so many of which related to Eric Clarkson. In retrospect, she realized that there had been, amid that strange silence in the hospital room, a growing estrangement between them. It was almost as if once the future cleared for them, neither could face it. Yet she asked herself repeatedly, surely if two people shared something very special, there would have been words of comfort, of hope, of the future, even during the darkest of those times. Unfortunately, the truth was no mystery. Rory knew of her love for Eric.

To assume that he returned it, however, had been naïve.

And in her newfound self-sufficiency, naïveté had no place. Therefore, coping as best she could with the pain of missing this newly beloved being, she'd determinedly shaped her new life without him.

Yet, now·he had appeared, suddenly and unbidden, threatening her peace of mind as only he had the power to do. In the instant, her heartbeat accelerated to a dangerous rate, and her knees weakened as they had so many times before in this man's magnificent presence.

"You've shaved!" she exclaimed shyly, grasping at the only sensible thing she could think of to say. Sure enough, his jaw was there, bold and strong, as she had known it would be . . . and stern, as she had also suspected. The same amber eyes, which had touched her so thoroughly in days gone by, now raked her petite form with definite impatience.

"That's one hell of a way to appear at your door, Rory! You never can tell who will be standing here!" Her green eyes widened at his rebuke. Was he serious? She had merely come to get her paper . . . then the sparkle in his eye gave him away, and a slow smile spread over his well-formed lips. "How are you?" he asked gently.

She smiled back, in relief as much as welcome. "Not bad."

"May I come in?"

Flustered by her own slowness, she laughed apologetically. "Of course! How foolish of me—please do." He walked past her gesturing hand into the living room, appraising the apartment while she stood with her back against the door appraising him. He was as magnificent a human specimen as she remembered—

tall, dark, and handsome, as the triad went. On this late fall morning, he wore a burgundy V-neck sweater over a pin-striped Oxford shirt, gray slacks, and loafers. A more dashing presentation she could not have imagined.

To her growing astonishment, he was inspecting her apartment with the care of the Secret Service, moving deliberately from door to door until he finally appeared satisfied. "I approve. Did you decorate it yourself?" Silently she nodded. "Very nice!" As she savored his compliment, he walked back to the kitchen door. "I'm afraid I've interrupted your breakfast. May I join you for coffee? It smells tempting. . . ." He had arched a dark eyebrow mischievously, and she couldn't squelch a smile.

"Flattery will get you nowhere," she teased, not altogether truthfully, "but you may help yourself to some coffee if you'd like. The cups are on the second shelf beside the refrigerator." He cast her a knowing glance in appreciation of her refusal to serve him, then poured himself a cup.

"Will you have some?" He was as thorough as ever in his observations, she mused as she nodded, and he reached for another cup. "It's on the table," he called, playing her own game, then he leaned forward from the kitchen to add, "or are you going to stand at that door all morning?"

Rory hadn't even been aware of her position. She was, in a word, astonished to find this man in her apartment and so very casual about it! Every bit of the love she had felt for him during those wonderfully exciting, finally heartrending days in the Yukon was there . . . and snowballing within her. He had, she'd finally concluded, felt sorry for her during Daniel's first, worst days and, out of that sympathy, had stayed by to give her support. But once Daniel's recovery was assured, Eric simply vanished, making no subsequent attempt to contact her. Why, on this day in particular, had he?

Confused and unsure, she forced a weak smile and padded softly into the kitchen. It was that very sound of her fluffy slippers that reminded her of her state of undress. "I . . . think I should get dressed." She felt strangely shy and self-conscious.

"Sit down!" He spoke firmly, though the smile that courted the corners of his lips softened his words. "I didn't come all this way to have breakfast alone. Besides,"—his voice lowered seductively—"I've seen you in less." Color flooded her cheeks and she looked down defensively at the breakfast, which no longer even tempted her. "Aren't you going to eat?" he asked humorously, reading her thoughts.

She looked up quickly, remembering the meals they had shared in the deserted log cabin. Wordlessly, she passed the plate to him and watched while he devoured its contents. "*You* haven't changed, I see." She finally spoke, only then beginning to accept the fact of his reappearance.

"My appetites are the same, if that's what you mean," he drawled between mouthfuls. "Any toast?"

Silently ignoring the dual meaning of his words, she got up and made him several slices. How strange she felt, wanting to tell him so much, yet afraid to. For he wasn't really interested, was he? If he had been, he would never have stayed away so long. "How did you find out where I live?" she ventured awkwardly, noting that he seemed not in the least uncomfortable.

"Some information is very easy to come by," he replied noncommittally. "I understand that you've gone back to school?" he asked, for the first time faintly hesitant.

So he'd been in touch with Daniel, she mused. But then, there was nothing unusual or surprising there. The two had become friends during their short time together on the glacier, and subsequently, the friendship was sure to have grown . . . particularly once Eric learned the truth about her relationship to Daniel. The only thing that perplexed her now was Daniel's silence on the matter. She saw him frequently, doting on him in her own, newly discovered fashion, yet he never mentioned Eric. Granted, there had been a silent moratorium declared on the subject and her hopelessly dead-ended romance, yet she'd somehow expected Daniel to drop a hint that he'd seen Eric. Perhaps Eric had requested it so.

"What are you studying?" His deep voice broke into her thoughts, its genuine interest pleasing her.

"I'm taking a journalism course. Just part-time. Then I free-lance for a local paper during the rest of my time."

"Daniel must be pleased." He studied her closely as he spoke, testing her responses. Had she gained the self-assurance to endure the comparison to her brother without a prickle? To his delight, she passed with flying colors, returning his gaze more strongly than she had yet.

"Yes, Daniel *is* pleased. But," she explained in a calm voice, "I'm doing it purely for myself. I've needed something for a long time. That was what last summer was all about." Now that she had started, the words flowed freely. "I was looking for something deeper in life, something within myself of value, a strength somewhere. . . ."

"And have you found it?" he probed gently.

She shrugged and looked down. "Perhaps. I'm not sure." Then she met his intent amber gaze once more. "I've reshaped my life . . . now that Daniel is back on his feet. I have this apartment, school, work. I'm actually taking care of myself for the first time, doing things which interest me and which give me satisfaction."

"What about fulfillment?" he asked pointedly.

Instinctively, she knew to what he referred. There had been no men in her life since her trip. At first, she had used her preoccupation with her brother's illness as an excuse; later, the establishment of her own life had become her major priority. In truth, she knew that no man would measure up to the one who had stolen her heart, the one who sat with her now. A sad smile preceded her soft words. "Maybe that will come. . . ." But her voice trailed off doubtfully.

"Well, if nothing else, you've become a great cook!" he exclaimed, leaning back in his chair and patting his stomach, which from all outward appearances bore not one more ounce of fat than it had last summer. "A far cry from canned pork and beans!"

Her light laughter joined his in remembrance of that first wilderness cooking venture. "That *was* awful!" she agreed in disgust.

"Not all of it." His voice was deep, his features serious, his eyes suddenly rich with emotion. Once again, Rory knew what he meant, yet her hackles instinctively began to rise. If he planned to barge back into her life, to use her for his physical gratification, then humiliate her at his will . . . she would have none of it! It had been too difficult to build a life with the memory of him hopelessly haunting her to ask for further complication and renewed agony.

"Why did you come here?" she blurted out, unable

to bear his game any longer. As much as she had deluded herself, the hurt was still much, much too fresh.

The light in his eyes dimmed as he stood up and returned to the living room. "I wanted to give you these." She had only been marginally aware of his dropping something on the coffee table with the newspaper when he first came in. Now she slowly appeared at the kitchen door as he approached, handing her a square package wrapped in plain brown paper. He said nothing as she opened it, lifting the lid to find a round copper pot, inscribed with delicately etched dancing figures.

Her breath caught in her throat as she lifted it out, raised the lid, and listened afresh to the mournfully haunting melody she had not, for a moment, forgotten. It was the music box they had found in the deserted cabin and converted into a cooking vessel now magically transformed back to its original form.

Poignant as the memories were, she cherished this and Eric's thoughtfulness in remembering her enchantment with the music box. "Thank you, Eric," she murmured, closing the lid and clasping it to her chest. Her gaze fluttered to his, then fell once more, as she struggled to maintain an emotionally even keel. What she wanted was to hug him soundly, to show her appreciation. But that would be unacceptable, she feared.

"And these." His voice surprised her, and she jerked her head up to see a long manila envelope in his hand. Putting the music box carefully on the counter behind her, she reached for the envelope and opened it. If he had been intent on inflicting pain slowly and torturously, he couldn't have been more successful.

Before her spread a series of photographs, maybe a dozen or more, taken on that fateful day Rory visited the site of the glacier. Tony had taken them, she recalled, as she studied the prints. Had she not known the characters, and thus known better, she would have thought herself looking at two people very much in love. Her brow furrowed. She and Eric had been preserved, for all time, in various poses of enjoyment: she modeling an oversized jacket while he looked on in amusement; he administering an assault of tickling which she parried in pleasured agony; the two of them, arms entwined in pensive silence. The glow on her face was unmistakable, for she knew it to be born of love. And she would have sworn, had she not known otherwise, that his was the same. Unconsciously, she shook her head, attempting to rid herself of the delusion. But it was only a renewed and deeper pain that assaulted her. The pictures were the last straw, fracturing her composure.

Shakily she walked into the middle of the living room and dropped the prints onto the table. Then, in a burst of misery, she turned to Eric. "Why are you doing this to me? How can you be so cruel? Don't you know the torment you've caused?" Eric's face bore a torment of its own, yet she was oblivious to it. "Why have you come here?" she railed. "Wasn't it enough that I've thought of you endlessly over the past few months? Oh, I suppose I should thank you," she whispered sarcastically, "for helping me to get through those days when Daniel was unconscious. My preoccupation with *you* actually gave me respite from my worry over *him*. Then, when he began to improve and finally cleared the woods, I couldn't even rejoice with a whole heart. Because, as he recovered, you retreated. And, for me, that was an almost worse trauma than Dan's accident had been. You were a much harder loss to live with—knowing it didn't have to be, knowing that I didn't understand it, knowing that I hadn't the courage to fight it." The hurt was back in full, the pleading. "Can't you see, Eric? I was doing so well. The ache had finally begun to lessen. . . ."

He had neared her at the last, his hands limply by his sides, his eyes fired by a spirit she could not fathom. "What ache?" he demanded. "Was the physical need that great? Surely you could have—"

"No! No!" she screamed. Then she shuddered, suddenly weary, her voice dropping to a whisper as she lowered her eyes from his steady gaze. "You don't understand!"

Two strong hands were at her shoulders. "Then tell me, Rory. Explain it to me. Fight it now!" She neither moved nor spoke, terrified of what he demanded, confounded by his need to demand it. His voice was strangely unsure, as he urged her on. "I have to know. Please . . ."

She could keep it from him no longer. Despite the humiliation she would suffer, perhaps he would finally leave her alone if she told him. The eyes that met his were dry, drained in defeat. The voice was tremulous, though possessed of a certain conviction. She knew only too well of what she spoke.

"It's not a physical ache, Eric. Oh, that's been there, too. I can't deny it. But it was minor compared to the other." She hesitated, shrugging out of his grip and moving to the window. Head bowed, back to him, she faced the moment of final truth. "The other is something I never imagined before I met you. I don't know when it started, but it was there in that deserted cabin . . . and has been ever since." She took a deep breath, then uttered the words, so soft and tender and heartfelt, which she had lived with for so long. "I love you."

A long silence followed her confession. Wondering whether he had indeed heard, she whirled around and then stopped short at the sight of his face. The features she had committed to deepest memory, intimately knowing the feel and shape of each, were now alive and vibrant, celebrating a victory she could not fathom.

Yet he spoke not. If this was part of his game, a game he had won hands down, then it had to be the most sinister game imaginable. To glory in victory was one thing; to exult in another's defeat was another. With the hurt throbbing as it was, Rory had nothing more to lose.

"I love you, Eric Clarkson," she repeated boldly. "If that gives you some perverted pleasure, so be it. But I'll tell you one thing. Even though you'll never love me in return, I've learned exactly what that extra special something in life is, and I'll always treasure it." The momentum of her words drew her further. "You can walk out of here right now"—she raised a trembling finger to the door—"and I'll still have those memories. Despite the pain, they were, and are, beautiful! Now, go!"

"I'm going nowhere, little one," he drawled, as his lumbering figure approached to tower over her. At her look of pained confusion, he explained, "I came here to give you something—"

"You already have, so you can leave—"

"Keep still!" he ordered. "You may think you know everything, but you still have a lot to learn. You are almost as blind as I was . . . until I saw those pictures." He pointed casually at the photos, which lay strewn atop the coffee table. "It's all there, Rory . . ." As she looked on in bewilderment he reached into a back pocket and drew out a small gift-wrapped box. "Happy birthday, honey!" he grinned, a look of unbridled excitement lighting his features and causing her as much puzzlement as the gift he held.

"How did you know?" she whispered in amazement.

"When I want to know something badly enough, I find my ways!" He cocked his head mischievously. "Aren't you going to open it?"

Rory looked down at the small package, timidly took it and removed the wrapping. As she lifted the velvet lid, she gasped. Inside was a magnificent ring, a pear-shaped diamond, mounted on a yellow gold band. Speechless and uncomprehending, she raised liquid green pools to meet the shimmering amber ones.

In a tone of unadulterated tenderness, he explained. "It's taken me a long time to forgive myself. I'm afraid I treated you very badly during those first days in the Yukon. I was arrogant, imperious, and jealous. I humiliated you over and over again; it was unforgivable." In another age, Rory would have loudly seconded his claim. But that was another age; in this one, she merely stared at him, afraid to hope, unable not to. Steadily, he continued. "It was wrong of me to want to hurt you, but I was insanely jealous of Daniel and then, by the time I'd digested the fact that he was your brother . . . well, there were so many other complicating factors in play by then that I was more unsure of myself than I'd ever been in my life."

He paused, that very unsureness measuring each word. "I think I knew that you felt something for me above the physical." His amber gaze caressed and calmed her, binding her attention to his deeper thoughts. "But it was a unique situation in which we'd found ourselves. Almost unreal. And very far removed from the everyday kind of life, which, even in my most active days, must form the backbone of my existence." A broad-shouldered shrug preceded his quiet confession. "Perhaps I was afraid of making a commitment . . . where my heart was concerned, at least. It had been so disastrous once." As though snapping himself out of a self-induced trance, he raised his voice for a new beginning. "That was . . . until I saw the photos. I know your face, Rory, like the back of my hand. That *is* love in your eyes in those prints. I knew, right then, that life would be meaningless for me if I never saw that expression again, or if I had, in fact, misinterpreted it. That's why I had to hear it from your own lips."

She shook her head. "But what does that—"

"Shhh. It's my turn to talk." He had put his hands on her arms, caressing them lightly from shoulder to elbow. Rory knew that as much as she tried, she could never be indifferent to his touch. Her eyes stayed glued to his as he continued.

"I'd had a very bad time before . . . I think you know about Donna. I was determined not to let that happen again. It was devastating for us both. I know now that for a marriage to work there has to be an equality of love at its root level. Oh, honey, don't you see? It's all there in the pictures! Those feelings, that happiness you said you felt last summer—we *shared* them. That's what made them so beautiful! I love you, Rory, more than I've ever loved any living soul."

Rory looked wide-eyed, from his face to the ring, then back again. Without another word, Eric took the ring and slipped it onto her finger. "Will you marry me, Aurora Matthews?" It was a brief second of staring at the ring on her trembling finger before Rory flung herself into his arms, clinging to his neck as he swung her off her feet. It was, after all, so right!

Their lips met in joyful union, a mere promise of beauty to come. When he finally lowered her to the ground, she answered him. "Yes, oh, yes, I'd love to marry you!" And she sealed her vow with a kiss that left them both reeling.

His own arms trembling with happiness, he pulled her down onto the sofa next to him. "I've missed you so, these last months," he crooned, as he smoothed her hair from her face. "I got the pictures from Tony weeks ago."

"Then what kept you away?"

"I had all of those doubts as to whether my interpretations were correct, whether I was reading a feeling into the pictures only because I wanted it so badly." Rory reached up and kissed him to tell him anew of her love. "But there was another reason," he went on, more seriously and determined to unburden his mind. "We both needed time, Rory. You'd been through a very serious upheaval. I'd sensed where you'd been, where you'd wanted to go, what you'd wanted to find—then Dan confirmed all of those things for me."

Her green orbs narrowed in lighthearted accusation. "So he *did* talk to you about me. But he never felt impelled to tell *me.*"

"Whoa, honey," he refuted her accusation gently. "I *asked* him not to, and he never, never mentioned the word 'love'." For that, she was grateful, though it all seemed irrelevant now. Not so, however, to Eric, who insistently proceeded to outline his own acts of the past lonely months.

"You *needed* to be alone, to do for yourself, to find
that inner strength you'd hoped for. Ironically, had I
known of your love earlier, following Dan's accident,
things might have been harder. It would have been
all too easy for you to form a dependence on me, hin-
dering your own search. And"—he stressed the
importance of his own impulses—"it would have
been much, much too easy for me to smother you
under my own wing, to offer my protection, my domi-
nation. But that would not have been wise for either
of us. I, too, needed time to work out some unre-
solved matters. . . ."

"Donna?" she asked, no longer afraid.

He nodded. "That first day, when I saw you in the
tavern in Whitehorse, I was drawn to you by the
uncanny physical resemblance. Somehow, I felt that I
was being given a second chance to make up for our
suffering, Donna's and mine. But in no way were you
like Donna. You made that clear from the start, when
you told me just where to get off!" He looked at her
adoringly, and she drank in his love as she unconsciously massaged the muscles of his back.

"But once I realized how much I loved you, there
was the leftover guilt to cope with. I couldn't,
wouldn't burden you with that!" He paused to lift her
hand to his lips and kiss each and every slender fin-
gertip. Then, softly, he continued. "Do you remember
that night when I woke you up to see the aurora
borealis?" he asked, a tenderness flowing from his
amber eyes to her green ones. "I told you then that
there were some things in the human experience that
we couldn't control." Assuring himself of the recognition of his words in her voluble eyes, he went on.

"At the time, I was referring to the chemical attraction between the two of us, the most obvious thing.

But I knew deep inside that it was much more than that. I knew that there was something unique between us, which could not be quenched by mere physical satisfaction. I also realized that what had happened to Donna and me was something over which, in the end, I had no control. That unique something was never there, happy as we were at some points . . . it just wasn't there. And there was nothing I could do to change that fact. As much as I kept telling you to grow up, it was I who had the soul-searching to do."

Rory had listened thoughtfully to his words, but her reaction was short, simple, and to the point. "I love you, my big, handsome rogue," she cried, as she shifted onto his lap and threw her arms about his neck.

And I love you, my beautiful, beautiful little one!" At that moment, she could not imagine what had ever bothered her about his choice of appellation. She understood, at long last, that a true loving and sharing relationship implied *both* dependence and independence. She could be his "little one," needing him, relying on him, and still be a very special, capable, and mature person.

When his lips met hers in burning embrace, she knew that he understood. Indeed, it was he who had encouraged her, both in the Yukon last summer, and here, during the past three months of loneliness, to become her own person. She had . . . and he loved her all the more. No other happiness could be as rich. She returned his kiss with all of that knowledge and maturity and self-possession that he had inspired.

"Eric," she murmured against his lips, her heart thudding triumphantly, "you've given me so much.

Now it's my turn." He drew his head back to search her face, so warm and willing. "I love you, with all my heart and soul . . . would you refuse my gift this time?" The current of passion that sparked electrically about them left doubt neither of her intent nor of his response.

Slipping a steel hand beneath her knees and one across her back, he lifted her in his arms and moaned huskily, "I am yours, my love. I can no longer refuse you anything." Effortlessly he carried her to the bedroom, easing her gently down upon the sheets. "You are my own Aurora"—he spoke in a hushed tone—"as awesome and beautiful as that celestial masterpiece. I will love you always." Then he kissed her deeply and devotedly, until they had ceased to be two, but had merged into one in a heavenly union blessed by love.